The stories in Jensen Beach's debut collection unfold menacingly in plain daylight. They seduce us into feeling at ease until the ground gives way under our feet. Here are people who hope to love and to protect those they love and people who fall down trying. Who burn down and stand up and heroically (stubbornly!) begin to live again.

— Noy Holland, author of *What Begins with Bird*

This book holds some of the most beautiful father and son stories I have ever read. This book is the father I never had.

— Michael Kimball, author of *Us*

It's easy to let a day, or a set of days, pass by; nothing is singular about them, or so it seems . . . and then you read Jensen Beach's wonderful collection, and you see how there is horror and joy, ugliness and beauty in the everyday, and you're missing it. Read *For Out of the Heart Proceed*, and then enter your day with better eyes.

— Lindsay Hunter, author of *Daddy's*

FOR OUT OF THE HEART PROCEED

Stories

by
Jensen Beach

"But those things which proceed out of the mouth come forth from the heart; and they defile the man. For out of the heart proceed evil thoughts, murders, adulteries, fornications, thefts, false witness, blasphemies."

—Matthew 15:18-19

For Anna

Printed in the United States of America.

ISBN-13: 978-0-9830674-9-8
ISBN-10: 0-9830674-9-X
First Dark Sky Books Printing, 2012

CONTENTS

Training Exercise

I'm in the backyard with one of my kids, doing what he's calling a training exercise, which is basically the two of us with flashlights, shining the beams over the grass and up into the night to see what we can see. My kid goes, "Pop, look at that." I look and I see that he sees just beyond the grass, about a yard or so behind the tree line—our house butts up to a small swatch of forest—a man.

It's late. Not too late, not even fully dark yet, but still it's definitely late enough for it to seem odd for a man to be hanging around in the woods in my backyard. My son shines his flashlight on him. The flashlight is a plastic lion and when he squeezes a lever on the handle, the mouth opens, the light comes on, and the lion growls. My son shines the growling lion flashlight on the man and the man growls back a very deep, shaky growl that comes from his chest. By now, I'm starting to get a little freaked out, because once I saw this terrifying documentary on PBS or Discovery or some channel like that about feral children and this man is making me think of that. I halfway expect him to jump out of the trees on all fours and attack us. The flashlight keeps growling and the man keeps growling back and the lion's plastic teeth are casting a weird silhouette on the man's face. We're all stuck there, locked, more or less, in what's looking to me to shape up like a battle of wills.

But then I notice that the batteries of my kid's flashlight are starting to go. The beam is turning orange. The growl is going soft, apathetic. The man steps forward, brushes past the trees and holds a branch up on the large pine nearest our lawn as he walks underneath it. He's oddly genteel about this. As he's holding the branch up with his fingertips just high enough for him to walk under without brushing his hair on the dangling needles, I see that he's wearing a dark blue suit and also that he's much younger than I'd thought. For some reason, hiding in the woods behind houses at night strikes me as the habit of an older person. But this guy, he's young. I'd guess twenty-five, but I don't really have an eye for age. He takes a couple loping steps over the tall grass at the tree line and sticks his hand out for me to shake. This kind of formality has always put me ill at ease. He squeezes my hand hard and says, "Nice to meet you, good sir." I try to pull away too early as usual, but he's holding on tight.

There's a tribe, as far as I understand it, in the Amazon jungle whose language does not include numbers. They only get as far as what they see. They trade large items, like baskets of beads and fish because they don't have the words to count the contents. The more I thought about this, the more I began to understand that I'm just the same way. If I can't see it, I can't believe it.

The man then takes my son's left hand with his left hand and tells my son, "Nice to meet you too, young man."

So the three of us stand there for several long minutes, maybe five if I'd have to guess, holding hands in an uneven triangle. It feels nice, a little reassuring, oddly, as it gets even darker and our hands all begin to sweat and the lion growls once or twice, I can't be sure, and the man smiles and we all smile at one another and there is light, so much light I don't know what to do with it.

Training Exercise

DIVINE MESSAGES

John Boy claims his tattoo of the Virgin speaks to him. Just what these messages are he never says. They seem important, though, because every time he gets one he stands up, announces its arrival and leaves. He makes us nervous.

The tattoo is on his left forearm. Above Mary's head is a small, burning heart below a banner with the words: THE IMMACULATE HEART OF MARY. John Boy is no Catholic. So the tattoo's origins are a mystery. But then, most things are with John Boy. This is why we stay friends with him. We all need a little mystery in our lives.

He's been getting messages for a couple of weeks now.

He tells us how the tattoo is teaching him new things. He's been having dreams, he says, and she's been teaching him new words. Like what, we wonder.

John Boy says: I can't tell you that. We wonder what the words could possibly be, what they sound like to John Boy's ears, and how the tattoo's lips move when she pronounces them for the first time.

▲

John Boy has grown distant. He's learned too much. We ask him to tell us what he knows. Fill us in, John Boy, we say. Approximate the divine, John Boy! We shout this at him every chance we get.

Our insistence has driven John Boy away. He stops by less these days, and when he does, he's melancholy and brooding. We try to cheer him up by pretending not to care what the Virgin has told him. But he knows our hearts now. She's taught him that. He knows how badly we need to know the content of her messages. And he knows that we will never understand.

For Out of the Heart Proceed

The Dark Is What

Lately we'd been buying old puzzles from the flea market. Any picture was fine as long as the seller guaranteed no missing pieces, which they always did. Of course, most of the puzzles were incomplete and the boxes were full of mismatches and deficit. People will say anything to make a buck. I knew this disappointed my son, but I never hid it from him. We'd just finished working on a pair of whales floating in a square of ocean. Jigsaw shapes of our brown carpet showed through the blue. "People can be greedy and dishonest," I told him. "You should get used to that."

Hanging the puzzles on the wall was my son's idea. He wanted to bring the outside in. I held the finished puzzle to the wall, said,

"Should the whales live here? Or there?" A thousand pieces waved in my hands.

He said, "Whales live in the water." He was nine. We'd arranged the puzzles by theme throughout the house. Vehicles we hung near the door to the garage. Water was above the television set. Forest, which we defined as any picture with the color green in it, was a long, thin row below the window on the far wall.

I squeezed myself behind the television among the dust and black cables. I hung the puzzle in an empty spot using double-sided tape and four nails I hammered into the wall with the spine of a book. "How does that seem?" I asked.

"Natural," my son said.

"We'll go again next week," I said, "if you want to."

▲

There was a sun like a thousand horses stampeding in dust. We walked down rows of electronic devices—VCRs, cassette decks, digital alarm clocks with built-in radios—noisemakers from the ancient history of circa ten years ago. I bought a clock that told time an hour slow. "We'll take this one," I said, "because it makes the days longer." The seller was a tall man with a wild beard and a missing hand. He pinched my money with his prosthesis.

"Why on earth would you want to stretch this out any longer?" he asked, and swept his good hand in front of him, covering everything we could see and everything we could not.

I was tempted to scold him for talking like this in front of my son, tell him not everyone shared his gloomy worldview. Instead I asked about his hand.

"The war," he said. He lifted his arm, showed us every side of the dull plastic and glistening metal. He winked at my son.

"Which war?" I asked.

"Pick one," he said.

Two women beside us had started to fight over an old popcorn maker. It was a heavy-looking appliance with a cracked hood and a melted side. One of the women pulled on the cord. Her turquoise earrings swung in circles. The other woman held on tight to the base. Together they pulled the popcorn maker into pieces. We all looked to the seller. With his good hand, he stroked his beard.

"Now you both owe me five bucks," he said.

▲

A low-hanging canopy of green, blue and black tarps shook and snapped in the wind. My son stopped in front of a table with a number of plastic VHS cases lined up in neat rows. There was a television on the table. Two men sat on folding chairs. One of them smoked. A pornographic film was playing. The man who was not smoking turned slightly toward the television and leaned into it like he was protecting it from us. A giant chandelier of a scrotum filled the screen. My son said, "What is that?"

"It represents one of many different types of love," I said. "Don't worry about the details for now." He took my hand. A woman's sad face appeared on the screen. She was a rare animal who understood her inevitable extinction.

▲

The Dark Is What

I bought two sets of playing cards. I bought an attachment for my garden hose that I was promised would double my yield of late-season tomatoes. I bought a book on the construction of the Hoover Dam. I bought a staple gun.

We were primitive man. We were inventing the tools of our own evolution. Gospel music played a few rows over and we made our way toward it slowly.

▲

We came upon a table of Jesuses. Hundreds of Jesuses on the cross. Jesus the shepherd of lambs. Jesus kneeling before a lumpy basket of fish. It was whole a city of Jesus. Each one of them was a different color. Some were upright. Some lay on their backs in neatly arranged rows, crucifixes head-to-toe. An old woman sat at the table. She held her shaking hand straight out at my son. "Do you know the story of Jesus Christ our Lord and Savior?"

"Hello," I answered for him. Behind her was a large sign strung over her booth with brown twine. It was crooked and printed with large black letters. TURN TO THE LIGHT! It said. Jjust below that: THE DARK IS UP ON US! I thought the error was funny but my son seemed confused.

"The dark is what?" he asked the woman.

"We are soldiers," she said, "for the Lord."

"I don't understand," said my son.

"The devil is everywhere," she said. I thought of the tables we'd seen so far, and of what I knew about the world, and I figured she was probably right about that.

"Well," I said, "fight the good fight."

I bought a purple Jesus on a cross. My son held it by the arm as we walked until he got tired of its uncomfortable shape and put it in the bag with our staple gun and the sweatshirt he'd worn that morning when it was still cool out.

▲

We passed old telephones, dolls, collectible sports cards, and car parts. Milk cartons overflowed with bicycle chains. We saw gardening gloves wrapped in plastic, athletic socks, and knock-off Zippo lighters. "One day I want to buy one of everything," my son said. "Just to do it."

This seemed to me like a good plan, but I don't believe in giving too much encouragement too early. It can spoil a person. So I said, "There's a world to see. Try that first."

▲

I found a record player. The seller introduced himself as Gus, but his hat said Bill. "This works," I said to my son and pointed to the device, "by a process involving a tiny needle in this part here, bouncing and sliding off grooves in the record, which you can see here. Think of a finger in a canyon making echoes on rocks. Isn't that right?" I asked Gus.

He said, "If you say so."

"I do," I said.

"Then it is," he said.

"Well," I said, "hang on. I don't know if I like your reasoning, Gus. What's more important: the right answer or how you got there?"

Gus raised his hat and scratched the top of his head with his thumb. "That record player is ten bucks."

"No thanks," I said. "Thanks all the same. I just wanted to teach my son a lesson."

▲

We visited the table where in the past we'd had the greatest luck with puzzles, but it had been replaced by something else. A new seller had moved in with piles of knockoff purses. My son wasn't pleased, but I reminded him that nothing lasts, which is both good and bad because it means you will never feel anything for very long.

▲

Even though our hearts weren't in it, we took a puzzle off the wall at home. We broke it apart and reassembled it. When my son started to yawn, I suggested we sit on the couch to rest a while. We sunk deep into the cushions. Outside the window, the heat left the day and the tree in our yard cast a long shadow. The first few of the neighbors' cars were coming home. We drifted off into sleep. I thought of whales and blue seas until our eyes were closed and the dark was enormous, and we slept a sleep so big it swallowed us whole.

How It Was When a Car Caught Fire on the Street outside My House Last Night

A car caught fire on the street outside my house last night. It came to a stop and four men got out and walked to the sidewalk. One of them made a call on his cell phone. The car started to burn. Flames tickled the roof, making the interior glow. Things got a little tense. The neighbors all came out. The fire lit up each of our houses. There was an awful smell.

My wife and I put on our shoes. I watched from the spare bedroom as the passenger windows broke. My wife waited across the hall at the door to our son's room for some signal that we might be in danger. She's always been the type of person who thinks a few seconds will make all the difference. It concerns me that her imagination does terrible things to our child, but I know she means well. She whispered across the hall at me to ask what was happening. I told her I couldn't see through the smoke. There was no immediate risk from the burning car. I could see that clearly enough. But I left the possibility of certain danger hanging between us. As these things do, it caused an argument about who cared more for our son.

After several minutes, the fire department arrived. We were in the middle of our argument when the doorbell rang. A fireman stood on the step. "All clear," he said, "but make sure to keep the windows closed tonight. The smoke should clear by morning." Then he noticed my wife had been crying. "Everything alright here?" he asked.

My wife smiled and wiped her nose on the sleeve of her bathrobe. "Sensitive eyes," my wife told the fireman. "Smoke's irritating them." The fireman and I passed a look back and forth—a whole conversation without words.

The fire was out. The firemen left. The police arrived and wrapped the car's skeleton in yellow warning tape. I explained this to my wife. She said she was too tired to argue. Clearly she hadn't been listening. That's the major problem with us. We just talk. We never listen.

The next morning, the police came again. They gave the car a parking ticket. I waited for several days for someone to tow it. My wife and I have since moved on to bigger, more important arguments. Nothing so far has threatened the well-being of our son. The car is still sitting in front of my house, its hood split like a giant yelling mouth waiting for me, or somebody else, to finally do something about it.

For Out of the Heart Proceed

PEAFOWL

I planned on naming the bird Profitt after my wife's maiden name. This I decided on my way to the living room. When I got there, I found my wife reading a book. I told her, "I'm buying a bird."

Without looking up, she said, "What sort of bird?"

"A peafowl," I said.

"Absolutely not," my wife said.

"You'll come around," I said.

She turned a page in her book. "That's unlikely," she said.

Locating peafowl is a remarkably simple task. In less than an hour I'd found a cock for sale about a two-hour drive from our place. It was a nine-month-old Indian Blue. When I called the farmer assured me it was a calm and loving bird. He was asking 500 dollars. "For another five," he said, "I will blow your mind."

"I can't afford to have my mind blown," I told the farmer, but I wondered if maybe I couldn't afford not to, either.

"We hatched and raised a true specimen of a bird."

"I'm just looking for a bird," I said.

"This is a pure white Indian Blue," he said. "There's a beauty in the way that doesn't make any sense. To the East Indians, there's some spiritual significance to the white ones. They represent the soul." He paused here and I heard him breathing. "To be honest with you, I might be making that part up," he said.

"I live in a small house," I said.

"It'd be a pity to break up a good thing," the farmer said. "The white bird is your bird's companion."

"How so?" I asked.

"I think they're gay," the farmer said. "Gay birds," he said and hung up the phone. My wife had moved from the living room to the back deck. I watched from the window as she dragged one of the deck chairs over to a thin strip of sunlight, where she sat and turned her face to the warmth. It was March and we were all anxious.

The peacock was on a turkey farm. I'd printed out a map so I found the place with little trouble. There were some difficult turns and once a street changed names on me without notice. But I arrived a full ten minutes before I'd planned. My tires crunched up the gravel driveway. I watched a plume of dust rise in my mirror. The farmer came out of the small house at the end of the driveway, shielding his eyes against the sun with his hat. There were a dozen or so horses in a pasture behind the house. I got out of my car. The farmer didn't remove his gloves when he shook my hand. "You found it," he said.

"No trouble at all," I told him.

He pointed toward a tobacco shed beside the house and asked, "Do you know about birds?" There were large gaps between the planks on the tobacco shed through which I watched dust and sunlight beam out toward the grass. There were a few patches of snow left. The door to the shed was open and in the brightness I could make out the shimmering blue feathers of one of the peacocks as it poked its head through the opening to size me up. I told the man the truth, which was that I knew only what I'd read online. "I guess I should have mentioned it on the phone," I said. "Is that my bird?"

"They take care of themselves mostly," he said. We entered the shed. Above the dirt floor, three peacocks were perched on a low-hanging beam that appeared to have been fastened between the walls for this purpose. One of the birds screeched.

"Here's your gay birds," said the farmer. He pointed a gloved hand at the two peacocks. The birds were sitting beside each other on the far end of the perch. "Take a look at that," he said. The white peacock hopped down from the perch. It sent up a cloud of dust. "Can't separate love like that, friend," the farmer said. "I told them you were coming."

The farmer helped me load the birds into the back of my car. As he said goodbye to the peacocks, he held each of their small heads in his gloved hands and told them to behave. I looked at my shoes on the dusty drive.

The birds honked and screeched the entire trip. I enjoyed their presence but did not want two of them. The problem of one too many peacocks is unenviable. I thought about turning around, going back to the turkey farm with the birds, insisting on my money back. But a man's responsibility is his own. So I drove to a place I know where there is quiet and open space. It's a nature reserve. Hunting isn't allowed. Of course I know peafowl are seldom hunted, but accidents happen. I parked the car and opened the back door on the white bird's side. He screeched at me. I took him by the neck and carried him into the trees until I could no longer see my car. There, I released him. I gave the dirt a kick in the bird's direction with my boot. "Go on," I told him.

Peacocks are intelligent birds. This one fanned his feathers and turned slowly around in a circle. He kept an eye on me as long as he could. Then he walked in the opposite direction and disappeared behind a small stand of bare alders.

Back in the car, Profitt had relieved himself on my backseat. I was angry, but the shimmer of his feathers immediately calmed me and I forgave him this transgression as I am sure he will eventually forgive me mine.

As I drove, Profitt began pecking at my shoulder in a way that reminded me of my wife warning me against some great danger, which is how I knew I'd chosen the right name. I began to give the bird a tour of the area. I said, "Profitt, there to the northwest is a reservoir that provides us all with water. To the south is the town where I grew up and where my parents lived until they died. This is what makes a person, Profitt, proximity to all this. Your new home," I said. I waved my hand over the dashboard, indicating the vastness of our lives.

Profitt squawked at me. "He'll be better off," I said. "That place is quiet and safe," I said. "Don't worry so much," I said. This set off a wild display of mourning. I thought of my wife then, waiting for me at home with her books and her patience and her quiet, unrelenting love for me. And I thought of the farmer, free of these birds I'd so willingly burdened myself with.

At the reserve, I parked the car and opened Profitt's door. He wouldn't face me and he didn't move. There was no sign of the white bird. I gripped one of Profitt's legs and pulled him from the car. His wings flapped madly. "You win," I told him. "You win." I set him on the ground and he composed himself, turned his long neck so that his head was tilted up to my face. Then he turned and pecked at the car door for a moment until he sat down on a tuft of grass, complacent and I believe mesmerized by the splendor of his new home.

RITUAL

My neighbor keeps birds because they are beautiful creatures and symbols of our Lord. Or so I have always assumed. He has cockatoos, parakeets, and all manner of exotic varieties I cannot be bothered to remember the names of.

On Sunday afternoon I brought my unread *Times* to his door. I thought he might need to line his cages. He thanked me with an offer to join him for dinner, which I accepted because I enjoy hearing people talk about themselves. I said, "When?"

He said, "What about now?" A bird screeched in a room I couldn't see.

We sat at the dining table, making conversation. He asked me how I felt about death.

I told him I believed in it.

"It's hard to deny," he said. He was a mortician. "It's not a simple matter of preparing bodies," he said. "In case that's what you had in mind."

I told him I'd assumed it was more complicated than that.

He reminded me that many cultures prepared their dead for the next world through an elaborate set of rituals. The Vikings, for instance, buried their dead in stone ships so the spirits might be transported to the afterlife. He told me to imagine a world in which the mortician was responsible for such a spectacle.

I pictured him at the helm of a great ship, navigating it between tree-topped islands and rocky shores.

He said, "Some people believe you can take objects with you. As a mortician, I can tell you this is untrue." He laughed.

I said, "That was a joke?"

He gave me an odd look, somewhat confused and disappointed, and said, "Not a very good one."

He disappeared into a back room, emerged from the dark hallway with birds perched on each shoulder. With a careful hand, he pulled his chair away from the table and sat down. The birds rocked a little on their perches. "Both of these birds," he said, "are named Wallace. I thought I lost Wallace the first. That very day I bought a replacement Wallace. By ten o'clock that evening the first Wallace had returned, and then I had two."

"The Lord works in mysterious ways," I said.

"What do you mean," he asked.

I told him I had always taken for granted that a man with birds was a religious man, or at the very least one with spiritual sensibilities.

The mortician smiled, poured himself another glass of wine, and told me that although mine was a fair assumption, it was incorrect. "Was I disappointed?" he asked.

I nodded.

He shrugged and the Wallaces released their grips on his shoulders to fly around the room in thick white arcs.

ORION

Tom showed up at work unannounced on a Tuesday night three months after the accident. I was losing another game of chess to the computer when he appeared in the doorway in black pants and a navy blazer with his nametag pinned too low on the chest pocket. "Surprise," he said.

"Surprise," I said, and quickly reached over my shoulder for Kim's cockatiel, Danger Bird. Before Tom barged in, the bird had been perched on the back of my chair, asleep, his soft breathing keeping time in my ear. Cockatiels are sensitive creatures. Even simple noises—a flushing toilet or a microwave timer—could wake Danger Bird to a fit of squawks and hisses. The opening door, together with the sight of Tom, a person Danger Bird had never been introduced to, released a flurry of nervous wing flapping and high-pitched screeching. Danger Bird avoided my grasp. He jumped off the chair and darted to the far corner of the room, where he paced, bobbing his yellow head from side to side. His crest erected straight back and vibrated rapidly.

"What is that?" Tom asked.

Danger Bird hissed at us. Then he ran back across the room and hopped up onto the arm of my chair. "Birdy," he said. "Pretty Birdy." Every time he was scared, Danger Bird said this.

"Doug, what is that?"

"This," I said, scooping the bird up from the chair, "is Danger Bird. He's a cockatiel. It's Kim's." Danger Bird jumped to the floor. His feet scratched against the carpet as he ran back across the room. He leaned his body all chest and plumage into his run. We watched him zigzag to the dark bathroom and disappear inside.

"What's he doing here?"

"It's a long story," I said. "What are you doing here?"

"I'm back," he said.

"What happened to three months?"

"If I have to take three months' leave, I might as well take some of it at work." He looked around the small office. Apart from the new computers, which had been installed over the holiday break, the place was about the same as it had been when he left. The gray carpet was still worn into white patches in front of the desks; and the couch was still stained from the cup of coffee Tom spilled last summer. We spent long nights in that room, waiting for rules to be broken, for something to need protection. For Tom, I could imagine how that might be better than home.

"Mum's the word," I said.

"Thanks for calling, by the way," Tom said. He walked toward me, leaned in and gave my knee a double pat with his open hand. "I'm kidding, buddy," he said. "I wouldn't have called either. What could you have said, right?"

"Right," I said.

"The change of scenery will do me good." I thought of the crumpled body of Tom's dark blue jeep. The endless line of cars they'd shown on the news the night of the accident. "You go crazy at home," he said. "Everyone knows I killed my kid. I can't just sit around forever with that." Tom's nine-year-old, Tara, was with him when his jeep blew a tire on the freeway. He lost control and the jeep flipped from the slow lane across traffic into the center divide. This was in late October. It was a warm fall and Tom had left the top off his Jeep. Tara was sitting shotgun and was thrown. I hadn't seen Tom since the funeral and even then it was only from behind, through several rows of the sobbing shoulders of his relatives. Kim and I didn't go to the reception. The birds can't be left alone for that long.

"No one thinks of it that way," I said. This was, of course, not true. In the weeks following the accident, there had been editorials in the paper and on the news about reckless driving and failing traffic laws. Even the *Daily Arrow*, the VCC student paper, had weighed in. Every time I saw an article, I thought about calling Tom, asking him over for beers, or to hit a couple buckets at the driving range— the kind of stuff we used to do—but I never did. I didn't know how to be in the same room as that much sadness.

The funeral was at the Episcopalian church, even though Tom and his family aren't religious. Tara went to school with the reverend's daughter. So the church offered to hold the service. The reverend was good. He played to the emotion of the room. It was a beautiful service. About halfway through, Kim put her hand on my thigh, rubbing the soft fabric of my slacks like she was straightening me out. "It's time to sell the birds, Doug," she said. Kim had been trying to convince me to have kids for over a year. This was a step I'd been fighting. My most successful defense so far had been her birds. We just didn't have the time or energy to care for both. But right then, in the middle of this awful afternoon, two or three rows back from the absolute worst-case scenario about having kids, she decided it was time.

Tom pointed to a lopsided cake shaped like the planet Saturn. "Was that for the thing?" he asked. Every January, a group called Friends of the Valley Planetarium holds a reception to officially open the planetarium for the coming year. We always got the leftovers. Every year, the planetarium adds a show to the season's schedule. Earlier that day they'd screened the newest, "The Orion Nebula." Before Tom showed up, I'd been planning on checking it out after Danger Bird had fallen asleep.

Orange frosting flowed down the sides of the cake, blurring the shape of the planet and blending into its gray rings. "I guess Saturn was what they could get," I said. "Want a piece?"

Tom rubbed his belly. "Why not," he said.

I served us both on Christmas-themed paper plates. Tom leaned against the desk in front of the monitor bank, tucked his elbow in close to his side, and ate carefully over his plate. He took large bites and chewed slowly. Danger Bird emerged from the bathroom. When he'd reached me he twisted his neck to look up at Tom. I picked up the bird with my free hand and rubbed the soft feathers behind his head with my thumb. He made a shallow clucking in his throat. "We had a break-in six weeks ago," I said. "You hear about that?"

"Anything stolen?"

Danger Bird pecked at my cake. I brushed him away. "A globe," I said. "From one of the classrooms."

"Who steals a globe?"

"Some kids. We're lucky they didn't get into the planetarium itself. We upgraded one of the projectors last month. State-of-the-art DLP something."

"Well, thank God for small miracles."

"I guess."

"The big ones never come, man. Take what you can get," he said, his mouth full. "This cake is pretty good, for example."

The planetarium sits on a plateau on the eastern side of the Valley Community campus. Below, the rest of the campus spreads northwest for about half a mile. There are excellent views of Arrow Field from the parking lot. The VCC Arrows have boasted the worst record in the state for several seasons. Before the accident, their improvement was Tom's singular obsession. We used to park the security vehicle at the edge of the lot, get stoned, and watch over the right-field fence as every team in the conference destroyed the Arrows. If it was late enough in the spring and it was warm and we'd smoked just enough, the light towers became enormous redwoods in an electric forest, and Tom and I'd watch as the maintenance guys finished cleaning up, drawing the baselines and dragging the infield. We'd laugh and listen to the wind and the darkness behind the lights, and when the towers were shut off, it was like the sky had been curtained over us. Before our eyes adjusted it was so dark we couldn't even see the stars above the valley wall.

Danger Bird softly bit my hand. His crest rose back to its relaxed state. His neck feathers ballooned out into a puff of white and gray.

"How're things at home?" Tom asked.

"Same as ever," I said, motioning to Danger Bird with my plate. "We got a new bird." This was a lie. Danger Bird was one of our oldest. For about a month, Kim had been trying to sell the birds, but Danger Bird's excitability was infecting the flock. When one cockatiel wakes up, the rest of them will. Without a full twelve hours of sleep, the birds were nervous and irritable. They hadn't been showing well and it had cost us a couple buyers already. So far only Monty and Lucille had been sold, which left five to go, counting Danger Bird. On nights before meeting with potential buyers, I had to take Danger Bird to work with me so the rest of the flock could get its sleep. Danger Bird struggled. I set down my plate to hold him with both hands. "They're wild when they're young."

"I read about the new show. Any good?"

"I haven't seen it yet. If we can get the bird to sleep, we'll check it out tonight." Over Tom's shoulder, I watched a car pull in to the South Lot on Camera 1. "Welcome back."

"Opening night tomorrow," Tom said, "I wondered if we'd get any visitors."

The grayscale car came to a stop in the top left quadrant of Camera 3. Tom immediately put his plate down and crossed the room. Danger Bird tensed. He said, "Birdy, Pretty Birdy." Then he jumped to the ground and ran into the bathroom again. I closed the door behind him before he could get out. While Tom made a note of the time in the log, I watched two people step out of the car. The figures weaved a complicated path from one monitor to the next, stopping every few yards to kiss and fondle each other. Tom pulled his cap on low over his ears. "Here we go," he said. In Camera 4, the figures climbed the left-field fence, crept across the grass and disappeared from view.

For Out of the Heart Proceed

The first year we worked the night shift, Tom developed a theory regarding the relationship between the Arrows' dismal record and the sexual behavior of the players. VCC players, he reasoned, were just getting too much action. Tom had read an article about boxers not having sex a week before a big fight. We were in the office, killing another empty night with magazines and computer chess when Tom looked up at me from where he sat on the couch and, like he'd just figured out some important truth, said, "Semen is the life force of an athlete." He then concluded that preventing its presence, as a matter of speaking, on Arrow Field, would surely turn the Arrows around. This was just as the team closed out their third consecutive last-place finish. One team simply could not be as bad as we had been for as long. As proof he cited the case of Michael Newman, the only VCC player in history to make it to the big leagues. Mike Newman was Tom's greatest professional achievement. Nine months before the A's drafted him in the fifth round, Tom and I caught Mike on the shy side of midnight with his bare, white ass tented in the air and pinned between the slender legs of Justine Walters, an eleventh grader from St. Jude's. Judging by Mike's reaction, we had caught him in time. We weren't sure, though, until Mike's season began to take shape. He pitched two perfect games and set all kinds of division records. His name found its way onto scouting lists all across the country. The Arrows made the playoffs for the first time in school history. Mike's big league opener was front-page news for over a week in the *Register*.

It was colder than I expected when we left through the planetarium's tall glass doors. Working inside at night will do this. All of your senses get recalibrated. "Damn," Tom said, and rubbed his hands together.

In my peripheral vision, I saw Tom's face light up with the blue glow of his watch as he checked the time. "We're lagging, Doug," he

said. "Speed it up. You saw these two come in. He won't last long."
We crested the lip at the top of the path from the Planetarium to the
field too fast and bounced in the cart's cracked vinyl seat. The motor
whirred as the cart picked up speed on the incline. In front of us, the
western side of the valley rose silent and blue into the night. Tom
drummed his hands on the dash.

We rounded a corner to a clear view of the field. It was a green
ocean held back by a red coastline of seats. Just below third base
the two were locked into each other, arms and legs snaking all over.
We pulled up behind the visitors' dugout. Tom flashed his Maglite
out onto the field, sweeping a wide path with the beam. The light
illuminated a cloud of steam rising from naked legs.

Tom took the megaphone from the floor of the cart, turned the
volume all the way up, and shouted into the mouthpiece: "Closed
area, people!" The kids snapped to attention. They gathered their
pants in their arms and ran across the outfield, laughing. Just as they
reached the fence, Tom yelled into the megaphone again. "Knock
'em dead tomorrow!" They climbed the fence and disappeared into
the darkness beneath the scoreboard.

I dug my hands deep into my jacket pockets.

"It's too cold for this," Tom said. He reached under his cap to
scratch his head. I took the path that ran parallel to the first base line
out to the South Lot where, according to protocol, we needed to witness the intruders leave campus.

On the far end of the lot, the dark silhouettes of the kids made
their way toward a gray Honda. "I recognize that car," Tom said.
"I know who that is. Jonas Powers. He'll be back at third base this
season. Fast, good arm, decent hitter, bad grades. Another season
here to get his grades up and he'll be off to a big four-year school.
Florida, Clemson, someplace like that. Head over there, Doug."

"Let them go home to finish the job."

"I want to have a talk with him." Tom sniffed and adjusted in his seat. "Strictly baseball," he said.

I drove slowly across the lot, listening to the cart's tires scrape against the cold asphalt. I hoped Jonas and his girlfriend would hear us coming and leave. As we got closer, I could see the fogged back windows and a slight bobbing of the car. I pulled to a stop a few yards from the car. "Let's go, Tom. It's cold out here," I said. I turned the wheels sharply to the left and gave the cart a little gas.

"Hang on!" Tom said. He was out of the cart before I managed to stop fully. I watched him jog to the car. I heard what I think was the girl moaning loudly. Tom turned around and put a finger up in front of a big smile. He reached out his fist and knocked firmly on the window. The car shook. I heard laughing. The overhead lights came on inside. Behind the smear of glass, the two struggled to cover themselves. Tom knocked again and one of the back windows rolled down.

"Good evening," Tom said, as I walked up behind him. "You wouldn't happen to be the same people we just asked to leave the field, would you?"

Jonas and the girl looked at each other. "No, that was someone else," Jonas said. The girl hugged her jacket tight to her chest and looked down, holding in a laugh. The light from the ceiling lamp reflected the white delicate glisten of her shoulders.

"Jonas Powers," Tom said.

"How do you know who I am?"

"Third base. Throws left. Inconsistent batting average last season. You planning on turning things around for us this year?"

"Yeah, man," Jonas said. "I guess so."

"You guess so?"

"Tom," I said.

"We'll see what happens," Jonas said.

Tom went for the door handle. Before I could stop him, he pulled the door open, exposing Jonas and the girl, naked from the waist down, to the cold outside. "Get out of the car," he said. He pointed his flashlight at them.

Jonas put his arm up in front of his face to block the light and said, "OK, OK."

"Tom," I said. He aimed the beam at the ground, where an oval of light danced over the black surface. I heard the shuffle of jackets. Jonas turned and sifted through the pile of clothes on the floor. He handed the girl her pants. She pulled them on slowly, leaning back against the seat to zip them. When they'd dressed, they both got out of the car and stood defeated beside it waiting for Tom's next move.

"Give me your keys," Tom said.

"We're going," Jonas said. "We'll leave."

The girl reached into her jacket pocket, retrieved the keys and held her hand out to Tom.

"What are you doing?" Jonas said to her, reaching for her arm.

Tom grabbed the keys. He tossed them in place in his hand as if he were weighing them. He lifted his flashlight and shined it down onto his open palm. "Unicorns?" Tom said, holding up a small plastic keychain with a picture of a unicorn. "Doug, check this out." He wound up, took two steps and threw the keys as far as he could, grunting a little as they left his hand. I followed their path, but lost the keys in the darkness. They landed flatly several parking spaces away just below a light pole.

The girl ran off in the direction of the light. "Dick!" Jonas said. The girl's legs kicked out behind her awkwardly. When she reached the keys, she bent down for them, one leg straight out to balance herself. The light was yellow and cold.

She put the keys in her pocket and walked back toward us. Just as she got close enough for me to make out the detail of her face, she stopped and took a half step to her left, put her arms up in front of her, flinching.

That's when I heard the slap. I turned around to see Jonas doubled over with a hand up to his ear. "Fuck," he said. Tom stood above him, the flashlight clenched in his right hand, while the fingers of his left, stretched outward, were wide open. "What was that for?"

"Tom?" I said.

"Shut up, Doug. I don't want to hear it."

"I fucking saw that, man," the girl said pointing at Tom. "I'm reporting you. I know your name."

Tom turned to look at the girl. He made a fist and opened his hand again. Jonas righted himself. He stood now leaning slightly to his left with a hand up to his ear and a grimace struggling on his lips. "Rachel," he said slowly, looking at Tom. "Let's go. Get in the car."

Rachel faced Tom as she walked toward Jonas. Her shoes scraped along the asphalt. Tom looked straight ahead as she passed and didn't break his stare until the car had left the parking lot.

"What was that about?"

"I don't know," he said.

"She's not going to report you."

"I don't know," he said. "Do you think I hurt him?"

"He looked like he could take it."

In the cart, Tom sat still, looking straight ahead. I swung wide along the perimeter of the lot, around the gym, and out past the tennis court. I hoped some time in the cold might calm him down a little. On our second pass around the campus, Tom looked down at his watch and said, "We should probably check on your bird."

Cockatiels are emotional birds, and Danger Bird had expressed some serious rage in the bathroom. I opened the door to find him standing in the center of the room, his head leaning childishly to the left. The toilet paper roll was shredded into enormous flakes that spread over the floor in a thick, fluffy layer. He'd knocked over the toilet bowl brush. It lay on its side, faint blue water running out of the tray. I grabbed Danger Bird and, like Kim had taught me, gave him a gentle squeeze and said, "No, Danger Bird!" He nipped at my hand.

Tom joined me in the bathroom. "Hold him for a second," I said. I cupped my hands over the coarse flight feathers and placed Danger Bird in Tom's hands. "Hold him tight but be gentle," I said. Tom held Danger Bird straight out, like he was afraid the bird would break apart in his hands. I knelt down and swept the paper into my hand. Then I wiped up the blue water with the paper I'd collected. Behind me, Tom said, "Be good, Danger Bird. Good bird."

I motioned for Tom to keep going. "Good bird, Danger Bird," he said again and again. I guided Tom and Danger Bird toward my chair and slowly took the bird from Tom.

"Now what?" he asked.

"Normally, he sleeps," I said. "Kim's going to kill me for this. This is supposed to be a calm environment." Danger Bird puffed himself up again. He shot his eyes back and forth between Tom and me. I put Danger Bird in his travel cage. Then I took off my blazer and draped it over the cage. "Sometimes you can trick a cockatiel into sleeping," I told Tom. I could hear Kim in my voice, lecturing me on the parenting of birds and children. "The cage limits his movements so he really shouldn't be spending too much time in there. He can get stressed out, especially if he's startled."

We stood together next to the dark square of Danger Bird's cage, listening to him chirp and whistle. "He's been disrupting the flock," I said. "I take him with me sometimes to give things at home a chance to calm down."

"Bird people," he said.

"They're Kim's babies. It was this or the real thing. I went for the birds, no question." I lifted the coat and Danger Bird sprang for the opening. He hit the side of the cage and let out a screech.

"Sure," Tom said.

"Shit," I said. "I didn't mean that." Danger Bird found his string toy and shook it violently. It rang flat. I thought of Kim at home with her pamphlets from the fertility clinic, lists of potential owners for her birds, six months of half-hearted sex that wasn't getting us anywhere.

"I'm not made of glass," Tom said.

"No, I know," I said. "I know that." Danger Bird chirped beneath the blazer and flapped his wings.

Tom put his hand on Danger Bird's cage. "We're having a rough night of it, aren't we, Danger Bird?"

"Kim's trying to get pregnant," I said. "That's why Danger Bird is here."

Tom ran his hand along the top of the plastic cage. He drummed it twice with his thumb. He said, "That doesn't make any sense."

I explained everything to him. I told him about the birds and their buyers, the tests and timing, even the names Kim had decided on. When I'd finished I looked down at Tom, who'd moved to the couch, where he sat with his arm up along its back. He said, "How are you going to get rid of the bird?"

Orion

"Cockatiels are expensive birds. Someone will buy him if we set the price low enough." I opened the cage and reached in for Danger Bird.

"Let him go," Tom said.

"Right," I said.

"I'm serious. I once read about this colony of parrots in a city park someplace. The birds escaped or got released or whatever and they just went to live together in the park. You'd be having a picnic and look up and realize you're sitting near a tree full of parrots. You should let Danger Bird go. He'd make his way. Wouldn't you, Danger Bird?"

"Kim would kill me," I said, but the more I considered it, the more I was certain I was the one who wouldn't let go of him.

I took Danger Bird out of his cage, cupped him tightly in my hands so he couldn't jump to the floor, and motioned with my head for Tom to follow me. We made our way through the lobby. The night reflected dark blue off the floor. I led us through one of the side doors to the auditorium. Inside, I hit the lights. Behind the cove, which was designed to be a silhouette of the valley, the lights buzzed to life, illuminating the gray dome ceiling. In the center of the room, the large black projector awoke with the sounds of the hydraulics testing their range.

"Wait here," I said. The control booth was at the top of a set of stairs directly opposite the projector. The staircase was shallow and thin, tucked close against the black wall to preserve the unity of the dome. At the top of the stairs, I turned and looked down into the empty auditorium at Tom. His upper body was hidden behind the bulky projector, his feet nervously tapping against the wine-red theater carpet. I ducked into the control booth and started the show.

The room immediately went dark. Danger Bird whistled. I rubbed his head with my hand until he relaxed. Small pinpricks of light gradually appeared on the ceiling. I walked carefully down the stairs and made my way back to Tom beneath the shimmering Milky Way.

"Welcome to the Planetarium at Valley Community College." The narrator's voice boomed into the empty auditorium. "We are pleased you are joining us on this journey through the universe." The stars became brighter as we approached. We panned left and zoomed in on the bright orange sun. The shape grew to take up much of the ceiling. It was so bright Danger Bird's feathers turned orange. Tom and I leaned back in our seats, sinking deep into the cushions. Danger Bird shook and said, "Birdy."

"Our solar system is made up of the sun and those celestial bodies that are bound to it by gravity. Including the Earth, there are eight planets." We flew past the familiar clouded-blue Earth. Tom buttoned and unbuttoned his blazer. "Between Mars and Jupiter, we find the asteroid belt." We slowed down. Our view rotated back and forth to demonstrate the circular shape. "Objects here in the asteroid belt range in size from dust particles to the dwarf planet Ceres, which is roughly the size of Texas."

"What do you think?" I asked Tom. "The new projector makes a difference, doesn't it?" In the darkness, Tom nodded. The view panned left and right. Tiny points of light grew as we got closer. "Many constellations are only visible at certain times of the year. Here in the Northern Hemisphere, Orion is most visible from October to January." Our view centered and Orion grew to fill the top of the dome. Faint red lines appeared between the points. The Belt shimmered brighter than the other stars.

"Seen from Earth, Orion appears to be plotted along a single plane. However, the bodies that make up this and other constellations are only connected in the human imagination."

Orion

Tom turned toward me. I felt his breath. "Did you know this?"

We aimed for the space between two of the brightest stars. "The stars that comprise Orion's Belt each exist at different points along the celestial equator. For this reason, they appear in a straight line from our perspective on Earth. Seen from the side, the stars are vastly different distances from the Earth. In space, time is measured in distance. The light we see has traveled great distances from the star to Earth." We backed away from Orion and circled to the left. As we did, the shape disappeared into the surrounding stars. Then we shot straight in. "The Orion Nebula is one of the brightest in the night sky and, therefore, one of the most widely studied." The nebula grew on the ceiling of the dome. Danger Bird scratched at my lap with his feet. Just as the milky orange cloud was swallowing us up, Tom stood. I turned in my seat and watched him walk up the aisle. Above his head the soft light of an EXIT sign glowed red.

At the door he stopped to turn the lights back on. On the ceiling, the nebula became translucent. It faded in the bright light. I followed Tom back through the lobby and out into the parking lot. Danger Bird shook in the cold. He struggled against my hands. I squeezed him tighter and looked back at the planetarium. The light from the dome reflected off the lobby floor. Tom looked up and scanned the sky. His breath filled the air above of his face. "There," he said, pointing west. Just beyond the tip of his outstretched finger, past Arrow Field and high above the valley walls were the three bright stars arranged in a straight line. I held on tight to Danger Bird and braced for the worst.

For Out of the Heart Proceed

AFRICA

The man and the woman were talking about Africa. The man's daughter, who'd been playing in the other room, entered the small kitchen, walked up to the table where the man and woman were sitting, placed a plastic toy in front of her father, and said she wanted a Popsicle. Only she said it, cock-sicle. The daughter had been having a hard time with the bilabial consonants. They ignored the girl.

The man had only just met the woman and was trying to impress her with his political knowledge. Africa was her particular field of interest. That's what it said in the profile on the online dating site.

The woman said, "As I was saying, Sierra Leone is a deeply troubled country." Then she nodded as if to say, aren't you equally concerned?

The man tried to ignore his daughter. He was on a date and the daughter's mother had refused to help with babysitting. The daughter moved a little car around in her hands for a moment. She said, "Daddy, cock-sicle."

"Oh," the woman said.

A minute or two before all this cock business, the woman had been giving a detailed account of a video she'd seen online of a forearm disarticulation. It was very graphic. The man was appalled, but eager to have sex. Because of this, he chose not to say anything about the violence. When she said, "Chopped off with a machete," and moved her hand through the air, illustrating the machete, he only said, "How awful."

It was awful, of course, losing limbs in such a violent, bloody way. No one could deny that. But this was a kind of violence he normally didn't think about; and here was his daughter running around on the linoleum floor talking about frozen cocks. He began to think about sin and circumstance and violence. It was all very disorienting.

"Is it her mother?" the woman asked. She had a concerned look fixed on her face. It was mostly in her lips, maybe a little in her eyebrows. "Does her mother use those types of words?"

The man looked at the woman and thought about his penis. It wasn't frozen or disarticulated or otherwise occupied and although this was a relief, as it would be to any man, it was also a little disappointing. He began to think of his penis as if it were a root from which his body acquired nutrients.

For Out of the Heart Proceed

The woman said, "Some people just aren't cut out for parenthood."

His daughter threw the car to the ground and screamed, "Green cock-sicle!" The man looked at the woman and pictured her as a farmer or a soldier or a slave—some kind of less complicated actor in a more complicated mess of events than was going on here—and he closed his eyes and listened for his daughter and all of her perfect mistakes, and he thought of blood until the woman said, "It's all so sad."

The man touched a finger to his eyebrow where he thought he felt an itch and said, "You have no idea."

Africa

In All the World's Oceans

"Sharks are found in all the world's oceans," Carlo says. "Even here." He has one hand on Lily's warm knee and the other on the wheel.

Lily is a bird. She's scared of everything. "I hate sharks, Carlo. You know that. Don't say things like that." She turns a page in her magazine. "Slow down. It's too windy."

In his hand, her knee is prey. Carlo bites it with his fingers. "Shark attack," he says. Lily is ticklish there but she doesn't laugh. "Grow a pair, Lil," he says.

After a minute, he pulls in the sails. They were making good time. Now the boat drifts and rocks in the waves.

Lily crawls to the pulpit to look at the white caps. Carlo looks at her in her red bikini and prays a little bit. Beyond her, he counts the boats on the horizon. One. Two. Four, Eight. They're white and still. The wind is steady and the waves are big. Lily is wet. The water on her back is gold. "I'm a miner," Carlo yells. "You're my mine."

Lily turns her face around her arm, mouths, "What?"

"You're mine!" he shouts. Lily's hair whips her face, catches at her moist lips. "You belong to me."

She pulls hair from her mouth with a finger and smiles. Water slaps the side of the boat like applause. "What is that?" she yells. "Do you feel that?"

"The waves. It was just the waves." From opposite ends of the boat they scan the water for fins.

For Out of the Heart Proceed

MASSACHUSETTS

The man doesn't recall the wisdom of emergency money until he finds himself in a parking garage without any cash and it's beginning to get dark. It has been cold all day because it's winter. This all takes place in Massachusetts.

There have been rumors of snow.

The man sits in his car. He holds the steering wheel tight. There's no telling what he will do.

He thinks of the dream he had the night before. In his dream he was lying in bed looking up toward the window. Another man stood on the edge of the bed. The man is tall; his head reaches nearly to the ceiling.

"Tell me your name one more time," the man said. "It's on the tip of my tongue."

The dream man shook his head and said to the dreaming man, "Watch this." Then he jumped out of the window.

The man shot out of bed and took two long steps to the window, where he watched the other man fall toward the ground. The ground in the dream looked exactly the same as the ground when the man was awake. There was a muddy patch near the fence. The man watched as the man pulled a string connected to a backpack he was wearing. A parachute flopped out of the backpack. It filled with air. The man floated down, landing nimbly with his toes a few inches from the wall. He said, "Timing is everything."

The man said, "I live on the first floor. How did you do that?"

The man waved at the man. He gathered the parachute and placed it carelessly in the backpack. "See you around," he said.

The man wishes he knew what to make of this dream. He has heard, or perhaps read on the stall of a public bathroom, that parachutes are symbols. He's unsure if these symbols are sinister in nature or gentle encouragements about the future.

The man sees a couple walking toward him. They stop at a red Camry. The man exits his car. He listens to the voices bouncing off the concrete walls and the tops of the cars. He approaches them. The man notices rust damage above the back right wheel well of the car and wonders if this means the couple is poor. He thinks: "There is no lesson to learn here."

The man gets close enough to the couple for it to seem odd if he were to keep silent. He clears his throat and says, "Excuse me."

He must look tired and worn out, maybe a little bit crazy, because the boy half of the couple says to the man, "We don't want any trouble."

The man raises his hands in a way that reminds him of an animal submitting to a larger animal and says, "I just need some money."

"Let's get out of here," the man hears.

"Don't go," the man says. "I don't mean to make you uncomfortable. I'm in an uncomfortable situation myself."

The boy gets in the car, closes the door. The driver's side window is open a crack. The man tilts his head and lines his eyes up with the opening. "Just a couple dollars." He puts his fingers into the opening. "Please."

The boy presses a button on the door and the lock drops into place. The man removes his fingers before the window rolls shut. The tires of the red Camry squeal as the boy backs out of the parking spot. The concrete is gray and shiny. It reflects the red paint of the car. The man watches the car as it ascends the ramp, makes a right turn he remembers being especially tight. The tires squeal again. The man counts only one other car on his level in the garage.

"Timing is everything," he says out loud.

He looks at the large number two painted on a concrete pillar a dozen or so parking spots to the left of his own car and begins to think that this is all funny and he smiles until he remembers that he's alone.

Massachusetts

DELAWARE

The man is reading about Manuel Noriega. He doesn't understand the Content of the article. There is trouble with the French. One of the man's eyes is injured. He's distracted by thoughts of the state of Delaware to which he has never traveled and for which there is an advertisement on the sidebar of the news website he's reading. Delaware is not our smallest state. His eye is really bothering him. The man is having trouble remembering just where Delaware is located. And the name of its capital city escapes him. Earlier in the week the man's eye was wounded in a minor car accident. At first nothing had appeared to be wrong. Soon he felt to the left of his iris a deep-reaching pain. He arranged to visit his optometrist. The piece of glass was removed quickly and without ceremony. He's now wearing an eye patch. The man worries his injury speaks mysteriously to some graver ill. Surely he will die. Manuel Noriega has not died. Noriega's figure and his odd boxy hat comfort the man. These things represent what the man is not. The French have been granted their extradition request. The man is relieved for this, though the pain in his eye distracts him. A spot below his eye patch has begun to chafe. He continues to read with his one good eye and his injured eye follows. He can feel the spot from where the glass was removed scrape along the inside of his eyelid. Manuel Noriega is seventy-six years old. The man understands the implication of providing the age. Noriega will die in prison. He'll never visit Delaware. The man, however, might one day. Dover is its capital. With this, he feels the pain in his eye begin to recede.

ALASKA

The wave at Lituya Bay peaked at 1,720 feet. The man is thinking of this during sex with his wife. News of the wave came in an email from his brother: irrefutable proof of the Lord's untempered wrath. The wave was a quarter mile high. His wife's belly is soft and warm. The man feels himself flinch—an involuntary pull in his left shoulder at the thought of the wave approaching.

His arm rises above his head. His wife opens her eyes, looks at him.

"What're you doing?" she says. He looks at the reflection of his right shoulder, and that of his wife's left thigh in the mirrored sliding door of the walnut-trimmed double closet, and the wave—all 1,720 feet of it—pours over him and he rushes to the bottom of a deep, icy fjord.

PRIEST LAKE, IDAHO

There's a man who lives on the outskirts of a medium-sized city in Washington state. His street is a cul-de-sac. His house is the one with the black shutters, which were replaced upside down when the house was repainted. Since then, the man has been unable to explain what it is that looks so strange about his house, but he finds, every time he comes home, a deficit in its appearance.

For a living he makes fine, artisan furniture. He specializes in rugged outdoor pieces. Accordingly, he owns many tools, all of which he keeps in a shed in the backyard. The house has been newly painted—yellow with white trim—but the shed has not. Dirty white paint is flaking off the walls of the shed in the rough shapes of familiar geographic bodies—Priest Lake in Idaho, for example, where the man often camped with his family. The roof of the shed is beginning to give, rot, it seems, from the inside out. It dips several inches at its peak, and a whole row of shingles has fallen into a dusty pile atop the long weeds. Or, if we decide this man is tidy and meticulous, replace the weeds with Bergenia.

The man's wife might be dead. Let's say that she is. She's dead. The pain is still familiar and, for this reason, confusing to the man. His work has been suffering. There's a stack of unused hemlock boards beside the tool shed.

The man speaks of his wife in the present tense, says things like, "My wife enjoys camping." It's not that the man has forgotten his wife is dead; it's only that it's become his habit to use language to manipulate how he feels. His wife enjoyed camping at Priest Lake in Idaho, and, if the man says it often enough, she does now too. She enjoys it. She exists in this enjoyment.

One evening in the final week of October, on a rare warm evening, the man is sitting out on his back porch. Depending on what sorts of habits we might choose to believe this man has, he's drinking a glass of wine, or maybe scotch, or maybe he's smoking a cigar. Behind the man, the fresh paint of his house glows warmly in the dusk. The back of the house faces west, and the sun sets behind a thick row of pines that mark the edge of his property. In the shadow of these trees, the tool shed appears filthy and decrepit. He's sitting in a chair he made with his own hands. The longer the man looks at the tool shed, the more he becomes convinced that it must be replaced. The painters had offered to paint it using the same pattern as the house, but the man refused. It's a tool shed, he'd thought then, it's supposed to look worn out. Now, though, he sees it for what it is. It's old, and it won't survive for much longer. The man recognizes himself, or some image of himself, in the shed. Like it, he is old and will, more than likely, not be around all that much longer. He's already lost his wife. His son—or it could just as well be a daughter—is married and lives back east. He's alone, apart from the dog I haven't mentioned yet.

Inside the shed, he keeps the means of his livelihood. Without his tools he could not do his job. There are dowel jigs, miter saws, and other, more fantastic, pieces of equipment. The man is wrapped up in this job. He makes fine furniture. It's what he does. Until one day it will be what he used to do.

He gets up slowly from the chair, goes to the garage for the gas can he keeps filled for the lawnmower he uses once a week in the summer, and returns to the backyard. Now it is dark. The pines are tall silhouettes. Or he might instead notice the orange glow of the security light, only just turned on, at the neighbor's house. He might hear a ringing phone from an open window, or a siren from a few blocks over. Some kind of sensory detail that makes clear to the man that the world is bigger than just his yard seems appropriate here.

The man drains the gas can onto the shed. He splashes the gas on the peeling walls. More flakes of paint fall. He might be happy about what he's doing, whistling or smiling, perhaps, or he might be upset, or he might not feel much of anything at all. Who can say? He takes a lighter from his pocket and looks around for something to light. If the man is a careful sort of person, he will go into his house and find a newspaper or maybe one of the old quilting magazines his wife used to get and light this first and use it to set the shed to flames. Or he will find a stick or a pile of dried grass. What is not a question is that he will light the tool shed on fire, and that it will burn to the ground. Smoke, first a thin gray cloud of it, but soon, when the thinners and stains in the shed become fuel, darker and

Priest Lake, Idaho

then black, rising acrid and dense into the sky. The man takes a step back. The heat is still on his face so he takes another step back. Then another. And another. In this way he goes about the task of building something new.

WYOMING

I'd seen a news report about a boy in Wyoming who was dying from some terrible disease. Maybe he'd been in a car accident. I'm unsure of the details. The important thing is that this boy was dying. People die all the time, of course, and it almost never makes the news unless the death is somehow unusual or horrific. The thing about this kid, though, was that it was Christmas soon and he wasn't going to make it that long. Strangers from all over the country were sending cards and gift baskets and things. Christmas in October. That was the angle the reporter had taken.

The other thing about this boy is that he and my son had the same name. It's not a common name, but it's not strange either. For some reason, this really struck me—made me feel for the kid.

A few days after the news report I decided my son and I should send the boy a card. I wanted us to give some part of us to this boy, sacrifice some of our living for his dying instead of my kid. I don't know. I guess it had something to do with achieving balance in the universe, re-calibrating the karmic scales, or something like that. My wife's always talking about achieving balance. We sat down to write the dying boy a short note. "Put your name here," I told my son.

He said their name. This kind of sentimentality doesn't tend to get to me—I've always been one to suffer more from nostalgia than sentiment—but seeing the name there on the inside flap of the light blue card, I couldn't help but picture myself the father of a dying son. Like all fathers, I occasionally imagine my child's death.

My son had just learned to write his name and he had this funny way of holding a pencil with his pinky finger stuck out to the side. He started writing and his finger was sticking out, dancing along like it was blazing a trail for his hand. Letter by letter he got the name down on the card.

"What do you want to say now?" I asked.

He wanted to know whom the letter was for. I thought about trying to explain that there was a boy in Wyoming who shared his name, and that this boy was dying. But the more I thought about it, the more I couldn't figure out how to put it just right, so I chickened out and said, "To yourself. This is a letter to the future."

My son looked at the blue card, then up at me, then back down to the card with a new kind of concentration. He gripped the pencil and stuck his pinky finger out. Then slowly he began to draw a picture of himself in the past.

TO THE WORLD I'LL BE BURIED

Ben sat on the edge of the bed, watching Molly's arms contort behind her neck and her elbows poke the air. She struggled with a button on her new top. "You want some help?" he said.

She turned her back to him. "The top one," she said. She held her hair up with one hand, swaying as if she could still hear music. A month ago, his Reserve unit had received its deployment orders. Molly had thrown going-away parties every weekend since. The parties started as a welcomed distraction—a chance to see their friends and together hope for the best—but the late nights began to wear him down, challenging his patience for his wife and her goodbyes.

In four months he'd be home again. He worked the button loose and kissed her.

Molly stumbled out of her shoes and gave a little laugh at him in the mirror above the dresser. "Laura's right, you know."

"She was drunk," he said.

"Probably. But there's a war, remember?" She turned and put a wobbly hand on his shoulder, bracing herself against him. "You're going there."

Ben saw the war everywhere. He didn't need any reminders about it. Laura was their only friend not in the Air Force or married to someone who was and her loud assertions about his heroics had been pissing him off all night. "It's a job," he said. "That's it, Molly. I'm doing what I'm getting paid to do."

She removed her earrings, placed them one-by-one in a small floral-patterned box on the dresser. "It feels nice when my friends are proud of you."

"I don't want anyone to get the wrong idea. I'll be sorting mail for four months. Nothing dangerous but the heat." Ben was assigned to a logistics unit. He expected to end up testing equipment and dealing with supply shipments.

Molly chewed on the inside of her cheek. "If you don't want to talk about it, fine by me." She took off her skirt and rolled her panty-hose off with both hands. "It's like a sauna in those things," she said. She tossed the pantyhose at the hamper in the corner. "Find the dog, would you? I want him to sleep in here tonight."

"He's fine where he is."

"Ben," she said. "It's an important step in getting him used to living here. I read about it online. There's a name for this. I can't remember exactly what, but it's very important."

"Molly," he said.

She pulled her blouse off over her head, unclasped her bra, and took a step toward him, naked and smiling now. "I'll be here when you get back," she said. "Make it quick or I'll start without you."

They'd had the dog for two weeks. In that time, Molly had set up a lavish play area for it in Ben's study. This annoyed him at first, but he never used the room and the dog made her happy, so he surrendered the study to the Lone Ranger's pillowy bed and drippy chew toys, and only felt anything about it when he remembered to. "Here, boy," he said into the dark room. The musky trace of hair and breath was faint. "Lone Ranger!" He listened for the tick of the dog's claws on the hardwood floor or the wheezy rattle of its snoring, but there was nothing. The dog was jumpy and skittish when people were over, and it liked to hide in unusual places. He'd once found the dog asleep in the narrow space behind the bed in the spare room; its eyes wide open and rolled back into its head. He thought the dog had suffocated until he nearly got his hand taken off when he reached to pull it free.

He opened the back door and called twice into the cold. Just after they'd moved into the house, when ideas for its improvement were still exciting and easily conceived, he'd special-ordered half a dozen railroad beams to construct an herb garden for Molly. Their heavy shape was visible on the far side of the yard. In June he measured a ten-foot-long rectangle out with four stakes. He tied a knot of orange flagging tape on each end. The tape now waved in the breeze like some kind of terrible reminder to buy a shovel and finish the job.

It'd been almost a year since he and Molly moved off-base. They bought the first house they looked at—a three bedroom in one of the newer subdivisions that seemed to appear overnight on the dusty hillsides. About a mile from their house was the shallow reservoir where three summers ago John Bailey, Ben's commanding officer when he was still active duty, taught him to windsurf.

He cupped his hand to his mouth and called for the dog. The motion-activated security light above the door turned on. He stepped out into the irregular oval of yellow light on the deck. Beside his foot, there was an uneven spot in the dark stain. He'd promised to add a new coat before he left. Molly liked a color called Bourbon. He whistled loudly with two fingers in his mouth so that when he came back to the bedroom without the dog, she would know that at least he'd tried.

The dog wasn't under the couch, or in the kitchen, or in the coat closet beside the front door. He checked not because he thought the dog would be in any of these places, but because he believed in exhausting his options. In the bedroom, Molly was asleep beneath the cream-colored comforter. The bedside lamp was on and in its shallow light he watched her chest rise and fall. He took a cigarette from a pack he knew she kept hidden in the bedside table.

Up and down the street, the leaves of the young Japanese maples that were planted in front of each house on the block pulsed in the wind. The night was cold for August. One of the guests had left a glass on the arm of the wooden Adirondack chair his father had made as a wedding gift. He picked the glass up and ashed into it. Just above the lip of the gutter, he saw the suggestion of something solid in the dark. At first he thought it must be the Lius' cat, which for reasons he'd never been able to figure out sat in his driveway and cried on cold nights. He clapped his hands loudly. But the shape didn't move. It was late, closing in on one-thirty in the morning—tomorrow already. He made his way through what might have happened. A drunk party guest, a fidgety dog, a car tire.

He dropped his cigarette in the gutter next to the body. It slapped and fizzed in the green water. The Lone Ranger's mouth was open, exposing tiny pills of teeth, which had before seemed vicious and judgmental, but were now only a reminder of how guilty he felt for having hated the dog so much.

There was an unopened box of thirty-gallon garbage bags on a shelf in the garage. He removed two, placed one inside the other, and then reached both hands in up to his elbows. He straddled the gutter and leaned over the Lone Ranger, covering the dog with the bags. Briefly, he checked for a pulse, but felt only soft muscle and the taut rails of tendon. In one hand he took hold of the dog's head. With the other he gripped its hind legs, pulling it up into his arms and turning the bags inside out. The dog was heavier than he recalled. He tied the four corners into a double knot and placed the bags into the back of Molly's station wagon. He reached in, pushed the knot down into the lumpy contours of the dog. Air rushed out of the bag. The outline of a single paw became visible beneath the black plastic.

The car smelled like air freshener and the cigarettes Molly claimed to smoke only when she'd been drinking. He tuned the radio to one of Molly's nostalgic presets and tried to concentrate on a song he vaguely recognized from when they were first dating. After a verse or two he hadn't known he remembered the words to, the bright sign of a 7-11 came into view. He made himself stop even though he knew they wouldn't have what he needed.

Inside the store, a tall redhead was behind the counter. She looked up from a magazine at the electronic ping of the door. He stared back. "Can I help you find something?" the girl said. She turned the page of her magazine but kept her eyes on him.

"No," he said. "Sorry."

To the World I'll Be Buried

"Don't apologize. I seen worse than you," she said. "You better hurry, though. We lock the fridges at ten to."

"Mr. Waddell?" Ben scanned the tops of the aisles but didn't see anyone. He looked at the redhead. Behind him he heard the voice again. "What are you doing here, Mr. Waddell?" He turned around and saw Vinny Liu, the neighbor kid who'd once or twice mowed his lawn.

"I didn't know you worked here," Ben said.

"It's just a summer thing."

"We ran out of beer," he said.

Vinny approached pushing a long broom straight out in front of him in both hands. He pointed to the glass doors of a tall refrigerator with the broom handle. "There you go."

"Right," Ben said but didn't move. He watched the muscles in Vinny's forearm ripple with each grip of the broom handle.

"Looking for something in particular?"

"Not really. No," Ben said. "Just beer." He scratched at the rough stubble on his cheek like he was trying to decide between brands. "Actually," he said. Vinny's red shirt was several sizes too large and hung on his thin frame loosely. Ben took a couple steps toward him. His shoes squeaked on the floor. "You wouldn't," he said, "happen to carry shovels?"

"Shovels?" Vinny asked loudly. "Serious? We don't have shovels."

"I need a shovel."

The redhead called out. "Five minutes." Ben looked at his watch.

"We don't sell shovels," Vinny said.

Molly always slept in late on Sunday mornings. If he got up at seven, he could make it to the hardware store for a shovel, find a place to bury the dog, and be back in time to make breakfast. The risk, of course, was that Molly would wake up hung over and suspicious about him being gone. Then he'd have to explain the missing dog and his choice to lie about it. He'd have to ditch the Lone Ranger some place that night. "It's your lucky night, Mr. Waddell," Vinny said. "If I get a shovel for you, will you do something for me?" His voice dropped to a whisper. He leaned forward on the broom, rested his chin on the handle. "I like Heineken. In bottles."

Ben looked at the fridge, then Vinny, then the redhead. He could see Molly's car through the window. Otherwise the parking lot was empty. One of the street lamps flickered. "Fine," he said. "When are you done here?"

"Just give me a minute. I'll tell Tammy you're my ride home."

Ben took a twelve pack from the fridge and placed it on the counter in front of Tammy. The bottles clinked. "Not too late, am I?"

"Nick of time," she said.

He waited in the car for ten minutes, watching the boxy green numbers add up on the clock. Vinny came out of the store wearing a pair of jeans and a baggy hooded sweatshirt; he walked to the passenger side. Ben rolled the window down. Vinny leaned in and said, "Come to the back. I have something for you."

Ben drove around the building and stopped facing a small walled-in area about ten feet wide. He could make out the lid of an open dumpster above the concrete wall. Vinny emerged with a flathead shovel in his hand. He rapped on the back window with his fist, opened the door, and laid the shovel across the seat.

"Where'd you get that?" Ben asked.

"We use it to get cigarette butts and shit out of the gutter in front."

"They'll notice it's gone."

Vinny walked in front of the car. His shadow was long and black on the wall. "Probably not," he said, climbing in the front seat. He buckled his seatbelt. "Where we going?"

"I'm taking you home."

"Shit, man. What are you going to do? Bury some dead bodies?" Vinny punched the air in front of him a couple times with his fists. He exhaled sharply like a boxer sparring. "You're in the Army, right?"

"Air Force," Ben said. "What's that got to do with it?"

"You guys kill people all the time."

"I haven't killed anyone, Vinny."

"Then why not just buy a shovel in the morning? Landscaping emergency?" Vinny laughed at his joke.

"Something like that," Ben said.

"OK, OK. Have your secrets. This whole thing, though," he waved his hand around the car, "this doesn't look real good. I'm just saying."

Ben looked at the clock on the dash. It was too late for this juvenile blackmail Vinny was trying to pull. "Alright, Vinny, you win. Know my dog?" He said. "My wife's dog, actually. The Lone Ranger?"

"Little wiry dog with white fur. What about it?"

"It's dead."

"Shit," Vinny said.

"It got hit by a car, I think."

Vinny turned in his seat, looked back into the darkness. "Is that what's in the bag? You're going to bury it." He cracked his knuckles on both hands. "Gross."

Ben thought about this for a moment. "It's the right thing to do," he said.

"Why don't you just ditch it someplace? Leave it in a dumpster." He pointed to the wall. "No one will know."

Ben put the car in gear and backed up. "It's the right thing to do," he said again.

The access road ran parallel to the highway for a quarter of a mile before it turned sharply to the east and met up with the road to the reservoir. Ben knew the road well. In the summers he parked his truck on the wide shoulder and walked down the short incline to the rocky beach, where he would pull his wetsuit up over his shoulders and assemble his sail and board. Just south of the reservoir, the valley widened and on perfect days the wind funneled into the opening, gushing so strong that Ben's board seemed to hover above the rough whitecaps and churning gray water.

"You know about this place?" Vinny said. "I didn't know adults came here."

Ben smiled at how young this made Vinny seem. He could remember existing in a world in which a public park could be a secret kept from everyone except your friends. "I guess they probably don't much in the middle of the night," he said. He drove slowly, listening to the gravel and dirt crunch beneath the tires. The cloud of dust behind the car glowed red and the uneven white beam of the headlights washed over tree stumps and brown clumps of grass. "You kids come out here often?" In his mouth this sounded older than it did when he thought the question.

"Yeah," Vinny said. "It's a quiet place. No one gets in your shit out here. Pull off over there." He pointed to a stocky maple beside two wide grooves in the dirt left from years of other cars parking in the same spot. He sipped at a beer. As soon as they'd hit the dirt road, Vinny had opened a bottle for each of them with the end of a plastic lighter.

"I can only guess what you guys do out here," Ben said. There was a sun-bleached picnic table and a wide fire pit that overflowed with ash and crushed cans. It was a clear night. They sat on the picnic table with their feet up on the bench, facing the water. On the far side of the reservoir, headlights rushed by on the freeway. The ripped twelve pack was on the bench between their feet. It shook as Vinny nervously pumped his leg to some rhythm only he could hear. Ben started to feel his drunk kicking back in. He wondered if he'd make it back here, back to the reservoir, to his surfing and Saturday picnics with Molly. It was stupid, he thought. Four months in the desert was nothing. There was a McDonald's on base.

"You're not going to try anything, are you?" Vinny said suddenly. He picked at a loose piece of wood that had curled up off the edge of the table.

Ben watched Vinny's jaw clench, the softness of his skin, the faint outline of a mustache above his lip. Vinny tore the strip of wood off the table, tossed it onto the dusty ground. "I didn't even want you to come with me, remember?" Ben said. In the moonlight, the maple cast a wide shadow on Molly's car.

"I'm not like that," Vinny said.

"Like what?" Ben asked. He took a pull from the bottle. The wind picked up. A series of waves overtook the rocky shore. Ben shook his head to clear his thoughts.

"My mom told me you're going to Iraq," Vinny said. He was looking down at the beer in his hand, turning the green bottle in the moonlight.

"Afghanistan," Ben said. "I leave next week."

"That's fucked up."

"It's a job," Ben said. He took the last sip of his beer and tossed the bottle. It caught the wind and whistled softly, splashing into the black water with flat tearing sound.

"I wouldn't think of it like that, I guess," Vinny said.

"I didn't think I would either."

"You scared?"

"Yeah, I'm scared," Ben said. He took another bottle from the box and held it out for Vinny to open. "What do you think?" Vinny finished his beer and placed the empty bottle back in the box. He took another, opened it and raised it to his lips. Some ash from the fire pit blew in a tight circle in front of the table. "Molly got the dog to remember me by. She said she wouldn't feel alone with a dog to take care of. And now it's dead." He looked toward the car.

"What'd your wife say when you told her?"

"All I think about is losing my legs. Getting killed. Last thing I need is Molly having some kind of premonition about it a week before I go."

"She'll notice," Vinny said. He pulled his hood up over his head. "What're you going to tell her?"

"Dogs run away all the time," Ben said.

"Yours didn't."

Ben stood up from the table and walked slowly to the car. He'd held bigger lies than this. Still, something about burying the Lone Ranger had convinced him he was betraying himself right along with Molly.

He put the keys in the ignition and flipped on the headlights. A thick whiteness enveloped the grass and dirt in front of the car. He picked a spot just to the right of the beam, a yard from the tree, and took the shovel from the backseat. He drove it into the dirt. "What do you think?" he called to Vinny. "This look like a good place?"

Vinny stood up from the table, took the beer and walked over. "What about the roots?" He set the box down on the hood of the car and hopped up next to it.

To the World I'll Be Buried

"I think this should clear us of the biggest," Ben said. He lifted the shovel straight up and dug the blade hard into the ground, forcing it down with his foot. The dirt was brittle, veined with cracks. It took a couple minutes to break through the thick top layer to the softer, muddy soil underneath. It was hard work and his hands ached. Vinny's feet dangled above the front wheel, cutting ghostly shadows in the overflow from the headlight.

Without speaking, Vinny opened another beer, stepped down into the thin fog of dust the digging had kicked up. He handed the beer to Ben, took the shovel, and began to dig. Ben leaned on the car and watched. Vinny pulled his sweatshirt off over his head. He breathed heavily. The pile of dirt beside the hole grew faster than it had when Ben was digging. In no time, Vinny stood up to his shins in a lopsided circle about three feet across. He leaned into the shovel and looked up at Ben.

"You could fucking bury me in here," Vinny said. He coughed in the dusty air. "How deep do you want it?" He ran his arm across his forehead, spit thick at the dirt.

Ben spread the pile into the wash of headlights with his boot. Dirt climbed into the air and hung like the weightless spray from a wave. "Deep," he said. He watched Vinny dig for a while longer, then circled around to the back of the car where he opened the hatch and reached for the dog. He knew there wouldn't be a smell to the carcass yet, but still with one hand he covered his nose and mouth. With the other he lifted the bag out and threw it the length of the car. The heavy package landed with a scrape just short of the headlights. Vinny stepped out of the hole. Ben pushed the Lone Ranger into it with his boot. He took the shovel and began filling the hole, tossing overflowing shovelfuls down onto the dog. Vinny watched as Ben shoveled. Soon a dark mound of soil rose from the dusty ground.

After it was over, they drank until the beer was gone. Vinny placed the box with the empties in the fire pit and lit a loose corner. The flame grew and was orange and green then orange again, and died out almost as soon as it had started.

In the smoldering remains of the box, Ben thought he could see how all this would end. He'd tell Molly about the dog in a letter. Tonight, though, he'd get home, climb into bed, and pretend that nothing had changed. In the morning, he'd console her, tell her that dogs run off. It's just what they do, he'd say. All week he'd hope with her. He'd approve the Lost Dog flyers. He'd even offer to hang them up around the neighborhood and on the message board at the supermarket around the corner from the house. He'd feel ridiculous about it, but as he pushed the pin through the paper into the corkboard and took a step back to see if the flyer was straight, he'd be halfway convinced that it'd bring the dog home to her after all. Molly would call him in tears when it happened. Everything's right now, she'd say. You're coming home safe. And he'd cry a little bit too, but not much, and say, I know. I knew all along.

They listened to an early morning commute show as Ben drove. Rain was forecast. His hands were streaked with sweat and dirt. At the 7-11, Vinny got out of the car and replaced the shovel inside the concrete enclosure.

Before they'd even turned the corner onto their street, Vinny had his seatbelt off and his hand on the door handle. His leg bounced up and down wildly. Ben pulled into his own driveway. The large picture window in the living room was illuminated with a light he didn't remember leaving on. He parked. Vinny half stumbled across the adjoining front lawns toward his parents' house. When he reached the door, he lifted a hand and waved in the direction of the car. Ben waved back and walked up his driveway.

To the World I'll Be Buried

Through an opening between the curtains, he could see Molly sitting on the couch with her arms crossed over her white robe. He opened the door quietly and stepped inside. He pulled his boots off and tossed them into the closet. "Where have you been?" Molly asked.

He looked past her down the hall to their room. His hands ached and his shoulders burned. The dawn had begun to sneak in, graying the lights inside the house. "Ben," she said. "What were you doing?" He closed his eyes, and with his tongue searched the inside of his mouth for the answer to this question.

WE CANNOT CROSS THE RIVER

We cannot cross the river until it freezes. Bekker predicts January. For food we gather leaves, berries and roots from the thick forest behind the cabin. Suarez boils what we find into a revolting paste we spoon into our mouths with dirty fingers. Winslow ate a spider he plucked from the web that now covers the ceiling and much of the north wall. We retreat into nature. We are swallowed up by it. A colony of roots breaks the tired plank floor.

There's no electricity. It's hot but the cold is coming. It's September.

Sadness thick as a river, and night you can write upon, forces Molineux to succumb. He grinds a rock into his throat and chokes a horrid, slow death. Suarez buries him in the soft dirt. Winslow whispers prayers. Bekker's jealous spit hits the tilled earth.

We wait. We are fathers. We can't remember. Winslow sings "Little Red Wagon" in his deep rattle.

Bekker finds a glass jar, blackens it with soot. He stalks the darkest corners of the cabin for dust and discarded web, for pebbles, for secrets to keep. He fills the jar and sleeps with it in the crook of his arm. When it's light, he peers inside to tempt us.

We have new feelings. We sit so close we feel our bodies. They don't belong to us. Bekker snores. Winslow cries for his children. We're amazed he remembers them. Suarez speaks Spanish in his sleep, crawling home to the womb he'll never see.

We're fathers. We came here. One by one to this cabin by the river. We cannot go back.

Winslow was the last to arrive. We are inevitable. We must move forward. Over the river. Past muddy shores and the twang of current. Bekker says he can see what's waiting for us on the other side. He swears it's what we need.

We must conquer. We must cross the river so we cannot come back. We are weak. We fear failure. We are pioneers of static expansion.

We remain. We are men. We claim what we see. We invade. We defend to the death our stakes in the dust and the dirt of our shrinking world.

Bekker's jar is full. He sits in his corner with it, unable to move. We are bones. We strike hard.

We collect sorrows in the room. We toss them back and forth until they are unrecognizable. We share them and they belong to no one. There is comfort in this.

For Out of the Heart Proceed

We feel the cold come. We count the days. We're less protected from what we fear. The leaves have fallen. There are new smells. Bekker claims to see farther than he ever has. He stands at the door of the cabin with his hand shading his brow.

We grow weary. We regret but have forgotten for what. Suarez has stopped feeding us, and we've stopped gathering.

Winslow tries his luck in the river. It's so cold. He will never go back. He's a torso. He's a head, floating on the black water.

We're in reverse. Suarez dreams of spring and thaw. He wakes terrified and calls to us.

We see. There's snow today. Bekker stands at the door, the open mouth of his black jar pointed up toward the hoary sky. A tree has lost a branch. Dumped its load of snow to a mountainous pile atop Molineux's grave. Just beside this, in the place where we raised a cross of two sticks in memorial to Winslow, there's ice.

We're impatient executors of our shattered wills. Two days, Bekker tells us. We talk about the other side. In spite of the cold, we keep the door to the cabin open at night and we watch, hopeful for a blistering storm.

We're on our feet. We're fathers. There's a light snow. It collects on our collars and in our hair. Snow sounds beneath our feet as we walk. We're electric. Bekker slides a boulder out onto the ice. It doesn't break through. Suarez throws a handful of dirt for traction. We agree. We are men. We keep our eyes on the rock. We follow Suarez's trail. The snow is wet. Soon there's water. We can feel the ice bend. It flows with the current. We are slow and all else is rapid. There's a loud noise around us, and we have nowhere to go. We cannot go back. We step. We know. And one by one we break through the thin ice and are gone.

We Cannot Cross the River

FAMILY

S omeone suggested swimming and someone else said that in this weather all we need is another incident. Someone recalled that there was an expression that perfectly explained this very moment. Someone said that yes they remembered it, lightning doesn't strike twice, and someone else said that as a matter of fact that's happened to a friend. Someone said that no one believed this story the first time and why should they all believe it now. Someone said that they'd read an article on the Internet about this topic and someone else said well, that proves it. Someone suggested that everyone calm down. Someone began to walk away and someone reached out an arm to stop someone. Someone turned and said they begged someone's pardon, but could they please release their grip. Someone struggled to hold on until someone else suggested that maybe lunch should be served, which turned the subject to food, which as usual had a calming effect. Someone prepared lunch and someone else set the table. Someone opened a bottle of wine and someone else accused someone of drinking too much. Someone lifted a phone to call someone about this and someone said, could you please put the phone down, lunch is served. Someone sat near the kitchen so as to fetch items from the stove and to refill dishes as necessary. Someone made a comment about someone's cooking and someone else found this indulgent, and someone else found it untrue. Someone said that it was raining now. Someone left the table and then the house until someone was in the yard and looking up at the rain. The storm was large and billowed in the distance. The rain fell light above the house, upon the yard, and on someone there. Someone pointed to the approaching storm and someone else remarked at how dark it had suddenly become. Someone said that someone had better be careful out there and someone else pointed to the clouds, now thick and black and seeming in some way to breathe if such a thing is possible, and the rain fell in enormous drops and someone started to run for cover. Someone saw a flash of lightning and someone else said that yes, we all saw it. Someone no longer appeared to be in the yard and someone remarked upon this change and someone else looked intently and rapidly at every part of the yard visible from behind the large window, which was now streaked with water. Someone else ran to the kitchen for a similar, but slightly closer, view of the yard. Someone sat still and hoped that someone was uninjured and someone else attempted to determine the likelihood of real life violating our most tested truths in this way, and as someone sat and considered this question someone seemed to recall that

For Out of the Heart Proceed

the expression someone had previously mentioned further qualified the circumstances of lightning striking one location twice. Someone said out loud that this was a variable someone had very foolishly forgotten, and someone else said that was no big surprise. Someone else said, what do mean by that? Someone said that as a family we're always forgetting important details, and someone else said, do you mean forgetting or ignoring? Someone said to look out the window and someone else did, where they saw that someone was now lying on the grass near the house in a wet heap. Someone said, did it happen? Someone said that it had and someone else said that it hadn't, and they all gathered there before the window in the kitchen through which they had all looked so many times but never together like this, and they looked for some evidence of the event they feared most. They looked in every direction but could not see the past because time doesn't move in that direction, so they looked for a long while and nobody saw anything at all.

Family

THE WEATHER FACTORY

From my son's bedroom window I can see the factory on the horizon. I don't know what kind of factory it is, but it has large stacks that release smoke into the air all day and all night.

Because I think it's a nice idea, I tell my son that this is the weather factory. He's five and, as far as I can tell, still believes everything I say. I point to the factory and tell him rain is made there. Those two large towers, just there above the trees, push the clouds into the sky. There's a man, I tell him, the weather factory foreman, who decides when it's going to rain and when it will snow. I describe this man.

My son laughs. He wants to know why the man works at the weather factory.

I tell him it's because of love. This confuses my son, so I tell him love is a giant heart that makes people do things.

He wants to know if the heart is inside the weather factory.

I tell him yes, yes it is. It's in a room just down the hall from where the weather is made. Together we think about this.

My son says he can't wait for it to rain again.

I say, neither can I, and we watch smoke rise from both stacks.

For Out of the Heart Proceed

THEIR FUTURE LOOKS BRIGHTER THE CLOSER IT GETS TO THE SUN

They spent their days in discount textile emporiums, only once paying too much for a yard of cloth. In the evenings, they sat together at the small table in the bedroom of their empty house, gathering the material, sewing it together. They passed months stitching together the fabric of their escape with industrial-strength string and clearance-table gabardine.

Eventually, their progress became too large for the room. The flowing waves of cotton and Italian linen poured from the table to the floor and out into the hall.

They moved the project to the dried lawn out back, running an extension cord from the window of the room to keep the sewing machine powered. All day long the wind blistered their lips. The sun dried their hair and burned their skin. Their eyes ached from concentrating during the near invisibility of dark nights. As they worked, they spoke of escape, each trying to outdo the other with predictions for their future. They grew impatient until they looked around at the dusty, yellowed earth and remembered why they'd started working on the kite in the first place.

Finally the work was complete.

Together they packed one bag with clothes and a small amount of food. They were careful to bring jackets in case the winds blew them north, where they'd heard it was much colder.

The morning of the departure it rained for the first time in a year. There were concerns the rain would create difficulties, perhaps prevent them from leaving. But they were both determined. Neighbors gathered around the makeshift runway in the park to marvel at the unlikely physics of the kite and its riders. They would take off toward the west, toward the sea.

As they unfolded the kite and prepared it to leave, the sky cleared. They said their goodbyes. Both were sad in their own way. Not because something was ending. They were sad for what might happen. And they were sad because they knew—no matter what—they wouldn't be able to force the kite to bring them back.

Each of them took a firm grasp of the kite's string and began to run. The neighbors cheered, dogs barked. Their shoes slipped on the wet grass. As the kite filled with the wind, it made a sharp slapping noise. They were both lifted slightly off the ground, their toes dragging a moment before coming back to earth. Just when it seemed as if they wouldn't make it, the kite gave a last violent pull against the wind and began to fly. Below them, the park and the neighbors and everything they longed to be rid of grew smaller. And when they could no longer see anything that reminded them not to, they shared a smile between them.

Their Future Looks Brighter the Closer It Gets to the Sun

THE SORRY TEDS

Outside of the town you've never visited stands a mountain. You've definitely seen it on maps, or maybe from the interstate that runs just to the east. It's hard to miss. In the shadow of the mountain, in a place that gets almost no sun, there are four small cabins. In these cabins live the sorry Teds. At first the Teds didn't understand what they'd done. They were angry Teds. They cursed you under their breath, called you names they'd rather not repeat. Then slowly—very slowly—they began to unravel the truth about what had happened. They want you to know that now they understand. The Teds apologize for everything. They're so ashamed. The sorry Teds almost never leave the comfort of the mountain anymore. They chop firewood and grow vegetables. One of the Teds suggested getting some livestock—a few chickens, a sheep, maybe a milk cow—but none of the other Teds knew how to care for these animals so instead they drive into town once a week for fresh produce and meats. The Teds miss you. Some of them are melancholy. Some of them are happy if they manage to forget you. Usually they can't. They think about you often. The wind reminds them of the way you smelled. Some of the Teds think you will always be springtime because that's when you first met, but others will always think of you as early fall because that's the last time you saw each other. Both of these assessments have detractors among the Teds. They all agree, though, that the cold winters remind them what it felt like when you were angry with them. The sorry Teds are not altogether certain you even remember what happened. But they can't forget and they need you to know. The sorry Teds are sorry.

SPACEPORT AMERICA

For a change of pace and scenery, I took my son on a trip to the Southwest. I'd once seen a program about New Mexico that intrigued me. The day we arrived in Albuquerque it was raining. I guess I'd assumed there would have been more sun. We drove south in search of it.

We stopped off in Truth or Consequences. In the parking lot of this little gift shop close to the 25, I looked north and saw that the storm had followed us down from the mountains. Charlie didn't see this and I didn't mention it.

We browsed T-shirts and key chains. I thumbed through a brochure for Spaceport America. I read a short paragraph that described the 2007 launch of the ashes of the Star Trek actor James Doohan into space. The same service, I read, was available to anyone for five hundred dollars.

Charlie was turning a mirrored display of turquoise necklaces. He found a necklace with a little obsidian arrowhead dangling from a simple beaded setting. He brought the necklace up to the register, where I stood holding the brochure open in front of me. He placed the necklace on the counter, spread it out with his fingers. The arrowhead was about the size of a quarter, maybe a little bigger. "What does this make you think of?" he asked.

The door opened. I could smell the approaching rain outside. I got the impression the arrowhead was supposed to trigger some memory or a joke Charlie and I shared, but I couldn't imagine what it might've been. "I don't know," I said. "It's an arrowhead necklace."

He looked at me. "Nothing?" he said.

"I guess not," I said. The only thing I could think was that maybe he'd once bought his mother a similar necklace. If there was some deeper significance, I couldn't locate it in the necklace itself. I looked at Charlie for a clue, but he just stared back. Then I looked at the necklace, laid out on the counter like it was being worn. "Listen," I said. "I want to be blasted into space after I've died." I held the brochure up in front of me.

Charlie took the brochure and opened it. He moved his lips as he read the description of the service. "Is this for real?" he said.

"I hope so," I said. The rain was coming down hard. We heard the rush of it. The storm was right on top of us. But when we looked out through the streaked glass doors, instead of the rain splashing down, we saw only rockets launching hurriedly into orbit.

FOR OUT OF THE HEART PROCEED

The day before he was set to move to Cleveland with his mother and her new husband, I took my son to the mall to buy his first winter coat. We'd just passed the perfume counter at Macy's on our way toward the mall proper when Gene asked if I knew what ninjas were.

"They're warriors," I said, "from Japan."

"Ancient Japan," he said.

"What's the difference?"

"It's the same, only older."

"I should have known," I said.

"A person can't know everything," Gene said and ran off, his shoes squeaking along the shiny floor. He hid in plain sight behind a plastic fern a couple yards ahead. When I approached, he gave me a wave like he'd worried I wouldn't find him.

At the store his mother told me to take him to, Gene picked out a bright parka that was a size too big. Immediately I made a plan to tell Katie he would grow into it if she didn't approve of my letting him get it. I was always thinking up excuses for imagined fights with her. That'd been part of our problem, I guess.

It was ninety degrees outside but Gene insisted on wearing the coat home. I kept the air turned all the way up. I started to shiver by the time we crossed MacArthur on the overpass. Gene sweat like crazy in his coat. His face was flushed and the long, wet fingers of his hair clung to his forehead. We talked about Japan a little more—he'd done a project at school—and he filled me in on the details of Ohio winters.

Katie met us when we pulled up to the curb at her and Robert's house. She opened the door to my car. "Hey, Baby," she said. "Say goodbye to your dad."

Gene waved and ran straight for the front door. When he was half-way up the lawn Katie said, "Gene, are you forgetting something?"

"Thanks for the coat, Dad," he said. "I love it." Then he turned and disappeared into the house.

"See you later, Genie," I called after him.

"It's awfully warm for him to be wearing a jacket," Katie said. She sat down in the passenger seat.

"That's what I told him," I said. "Are you all packed? Got the pre-move jitters?"

"Just clothes left. And one last trip to the Salvation Army. It's been a lot of work."

"Glad it's not me," I said.

She reached her hand out and touched the latch on the glove compartment with her finger, squeezing it open and closed. "How're you doing with all this?"

"I'm OK. I'll miss Gene, of course."

"I can't tell you how grateful we are that you agreed to this," Katie said. Her husband, Robert, was moving them to Cleveland for a new job. Robert had worked as an air traffic controller at SFO for as long as I'd known him. In the last year, budget cuts threatened his job. Finally, a switch to working nights had sent him out looking for someplace new. Cleveland was the only airport to make an offer. "Distance is so arbitrary these days, don't you think?" Katie said. "Robert's brother commutes to Phoenix from Pittsburgh. He's a pilot. Can you believe that?"

"Unbelievable," I said.

"Anyway, I just wanted to tell you again that you're welcome anytime," she said and touched my knee. "I know it seems far, but we'd be happy to have you."

"Good to know."

Katie got out of the car. She leaned into the open door.

"I'd like to swing by tomorrow to say good bye," I said. "What time is your flight?"

"We don't have to leave until mid-afternoon. You can get Gene out of my hair while we finish up with the packing." The movers had been there the day before and taken the furniture and cars. There was a rental in the driveway.

"I have to take Ted to work at nine," I said.

"It's too bad you never managed that kind of dedication with me."

"Katie," I said, but stopped myself. "I'll see you tomorrow."

Katie put her knee on the passenger seat, and reached her hand

For Out of the Heart Proceed

into the car, placing the tips of her fingers gently on my shoulder. We both looked at where she was touching me. "Jim," she said, "how are you really?"

"What do you mean?"

"I'd be a mess. It's like you don't even care." I knew Katie had expected to have to fight harder for this move. For the past few months she'd been treating me like I had some secret legal trump card I was going to throw down at the last minute to make Gene stay. I didn't, and even if I had I wouldn't have used it. I think maybe I knew he was better off. That sounds defeatist, I know, but really, where was I going? Gene had Cleveland and his mother and Robert. It was lined up for him. There were probably good schools out there. The winters didn't sound like much fun, of course, but in a way I think I was excited for him. I like new starts. I'm just never able to give myself any. "Like you say, distance isn't such a big deal anymore. This is going to be good for Gene. I'm happy for him."

"OK," she said and backed away from the car with her arms up in front of her like she was surrendering to some great offense. "You don't owe it to me to talk about it."

▲

When I got home Ted was in the front yard washing our landlady's car. Estelle is always giving Ted odd jobs like this. She sat on the porch, reading a magazine. Ted waved a soapy sponge at me as I pulled up to the curb. Estelle's car was streaked with dried soapsuds. He'd left the hose running. The lawn was a muddy swamp of frothy water.

During the sixteen years I'd been living in the Pink Lady, which is what Ted called the large pink Victorian in north Oakland where we lived, I'd slowly been put in charge of Ted. He was epileptic and couldn't drive, so I took him to appointments and to check in with his social worker. Three days a week I dropped him off at the Best Buy in Emeryville, where he repaired computers. About a decade ago, Ted started taking night classes at Laney College. Three days a week during the school year I'd drive him back and forth from campus and the Pink Lady, the back seat of my car full of bad sculpture or astronomy books or whatever Ted was taking that quarter. He sometimes gave me gas money, but mostly he paid me in meals he'd learned how to prepare at one or the other of his cooking classes. Over the years, I guess we got pretty close.

"Señor Jimmy!" he said. That quarter Ted was taking Conversational Spanish II. Early on I'd made the mistake of mentioning that I took Spanish in high school, and since then Ted had begun every one of our conversations with a new Spanish phrase. "¡Tanto tiempo sinverte!" he said.

"I don't remember what that means."

"Long time no see," he said and looked at me like I might, magically, start speaking Spanish back to him.

"We saw each other this morning."

"¿Cómo está usted?"

"Pretty good."

"That's good to hear, Jim."

"The car looks about done," I said.

"Over and out!" Ted made a series of robotic, musical beeps and moved his arms and legs mechanically, popping and jerking across the flooded lawn. Soapsuds flew off the sponge in rabid arcs.

For Out of the Heart Proceed

As I went for my keys Ted called out, "The robot is lonely, Jimmy! Join me in a dance!"

"Rain check, Ted."

"Good afternoon," Estelle said as I approached the porch. She fanned herself with her magazine. "It's a hot one today."

"Hi, Estelle. Putting Ted to work as usual, I see."

"James," she said, "as I've told you before, people like Ted need to feel like they are being put to good use. And my car needed a wash. This would be what some folks call a win-win situation. Good for Ted's self-esteem and good for my car." Estelle stood up and came to the porch railing. She leaned her left hip into it for balance. Her blouse was an unnatural bright green dotted with small white flowers. On Estelle's frame it gave the impression that she was standing behind an enormous fake plant.

"He's going to flood the lawn, Estelle. You should let him stop."

"Rough day, sweetie?" Estelle asked. She pulled at the hem of her blouse and fanned her face harder with the magazine. I could just make out a small, dark patch of sweat forming between her sizable breasts. "You look tired."

"About average."

"When does the boy leave?" she asked.

"Tomorrow."

"So soon," she said. "Don't you worry. They'll be back. Nobody ever leaves California for good. Believe me, I've tried."

"Thanks," I said and walked down the steps to my front door. I unlocked it, reached down, and picked up the mail from the hall. I flipped through the envelopes and advertisements, scanning for Cleveland return addresses. It already felt like a habit. There was a card from Robert and Katie. I tore open the envelope with my house key. On the front of the card, in light blue lettering, it said, "Just wanted to say . . ." I opened it. Inside it read, "Thanks for Being You!" Underneath that, Robert had signed both of their names.

Around eleven, Ted walked in without knocking. I had the news on. "Buenos tardes, Jim," he said. "I was thinking. What about me and you driving out to see Gene at Thanksgiving."

"I don't think so, Ted."

"Thanksgiving with your kid," he said. "What's more thankful than that?"

The news went to commercial and I muted the TV. "I might go in the new year."

"It's a sad thing, Jimmy," he said.

"I guess it is."

Ted picked up the card and flipped it over a couple times. "What is this?"

"It's a card from Katie and Robert," I said.

"I didn't know they made a card for 'Thanks for letting us steal your kid.'"

"Funny."

Ted poured himself a glass of water from the faucet. "Either way, I think you got the shit end of it," he said. He sat down and positioned himself in the middle of the couch, taking the remote control, and switching to a classic movie channel. His stretched his arms out along the back of the couch. An old Western was on. The hollow echoes of fake galloping filled the room.

I got up and went to the refrigerator for another beer. "You washed Estelle's car again this afternoon," I said. "You know she thinks you're retarded, right?"

"She pays me."

"Money?"

"I think it makes her feel good about herself. Helping the less fortunate."

I took the card from the counter, lit the stove, and placed the corner of the card in the blue flame. It caught faster than I'd expected, sending a plume of black smoke up into the vent. The fire ate away at the card in an uneven, smoldering line of bright orange. When I couldn't hold it anymore I tossed it in the sink and turned the faucet on. The Western went to commercial. Without turning to look at me, Ted said, "Does that feel better?"

▲

I knocked on Ted's door at eight the next morning. He wasn't wearing pants when he answered the door. "Buenos dias," he said.

"You ready to go?"

"Where are we going?"

"Don't you work today?"

"At ten-thirty."

"Ted, you told me you started at nine."

"I get off at nine. In the post meridian. I'm working a double today. Summer vacations have gummed up the system."

"We'll have to pick Gene up on the way," I said. "I want to spend the morning with him before his flight. We'll drop you off, then Gene and I can go do something."

"Roger, Jim," he said. "What are you guys going to do?"

"Put your pants on, Ted."

At the car, Ted climbed into the back seat. "What are you doing?" I asked.

"Gene's got shotgun," he said.

"But you don't need to sit in the back now, Ted."

"Que te mejores pronto," he said. "Feel better soon, amigo."

There was traffic on 580. Ted and I got strange looks. We pulled up to Katie and Robert's house at a quarter to nine. Ted reached over the backseat toward the steering wheel. "What are you doing?" I asked, and pushed his arm away.

"Honk the horn. Gene will be alerted of our arrival."

I picked my phone up from the center console and scrolled down the contacts list until I got to K. "Katie?" I said into the phone. "Am I too early to see Gene?"

"Hi, Jim. You're not too early at all. I'll send Gene out. You're being such a big help. You should know that." I looked up at the house. Weeds grew wild below the long window of the family room. Robert came to the window. He cupped his hand to it and leaned forward. The morning was bright and he squinted.

"Oh," Katie said as she appeared next to Robert, "We see you. Hi, Jim." Katie pointed at my car. "There's Jim, Robert." They both waved.

Ted and I waved back. "I'll go see if Gene is ready," Katie said.

"What's happening?" Ted asked. Katie walked away from the window and disappeared into the dark room behind her. Robert waved again and smiled. He lifted his coffee cup toward us and nodded his head, and then turned and followed Katie away from the window.

"Did you see that?" Ted asked.

"See what?"

"The thirty cent smile, Jimmy. Cheap and slimy."

"He smiled, Ted."

"Exactly," he said. "He should be out here telling you he's sorry. He's stealing your kid, man, and you're not doing anything about it. You're just sitting there like a toad."

For Out of the Heart Proceed

"A toad?"

"A big, lazy toad," he said. "¡Mierda!"

Ted got out of my car and walked quickly toward Robert's rental. He looked up at the house and back at me. Then he unzipped and pissed all over the rental car's bumper. He rocked his hips from side to side and thrust his pelvis back and forth. He raised his left fist, pumping it in the air a couple times. The urine collected in a delta at his feet. When he'd finished, he turned to watch the stream trickle down the driveway, zipped his pants, stepped over the stream, and walked slowly back to the car. He got in the backseat and buckled his seatbelt.

"Ted," I said into the rearview mirror. "What was that?"

"Great, huh?"

"You don't get it," I said, "I lost. And I can't do anything about it. Gene's going to have a go of it away from me and shit like what you just did. I'm happy he's going."

"You're going to choke on a lie like that."

I scanned through the radio presets, imagining it was my job to guide the mess of sounds safely to land, each note and crackle of the radio a clear instruction to an approaching plane.

Gene came out and shuffled across the lawn toward the car. "Hi, Genie," I said as he climbed in the front seat.

Before I could tell him to buckle himself in, he turned to look around the headrest at Ted.

"Hi, Buddy," Ted said, "Ready for the big move?"

"I guess," Gene said.

"Buckle up."

"So, Genie, serious question," Ted said as we pulled up at the traffic light at the end of Katie's street. "Have you made up your mind about the Browns?"

For Out of the Heart Proceed

"What are the Browns?" Gene asked.

In the rearview mirror I watched as Ted put two fingers up to his temple. He pulled the trigger and let his chin fall to his chest. "This is what happens when a boy grows up without a father," he said. Gene looked around his seat, straining to see Ted. "What's happening back there, Ted?" he asked.

"Gene," he said, looking up and right at him, "I was just wondering. Do you know anything about robots?"

"Do you?" Gene said.

"Only everything there is to know."

"How come?" Gene asked.

"Your dad hasn't told you?"

"What?"

"The three of us. We're robots from another galaxy."

"No, we're not," Gene said. "Robots don't come from space."

"We anticipated this answer," Ted said. "Tell him, Jimmy."

Gene pulled at his seatbelt. He rubbed his shoes together.

"Ted's right." I opened my eyes as wide as I could and stiffly turned my neck to look at Gene. "Robots," I said.

"And another thing. Electronics stores are where robots like us live when they first arrive to Earth. You may have noticed I have been unable to leave the comfort of Best Buy, for instance. By nature, I am a homesick person."

"That's not true," Gene said, and looked back between the seats at Ted, who was now sitting in the middle and drumming the center console with two fingers along with the faint static of music on the radio.

"Eventually someone comes to buy us and we go home with them, where we grow into our human form. Think about it." I took Telegraph to Broadway, all the way to Jack London Square, then

For Out of the Heart Proceed

back up through Chinatown and around the lake. He wasn't paying any attention, but I was giving Gene a last tour of our city. Ted hummed along with the radio.

At Ted's work, I pulled up to the fire lane and put the car in park. Indistinct waves of heat rose from the asphalt. "Gene," Ted said, "you take care of yourself and come visit me sometime. See you at nine, Jim?" He touched Gene's head as he climbed out of the backseat. Gene waved and kept his hand up against the window until Ted disappeared into the store.

"Let's take a drive, Genie. What do you think? Want to go out to the marina and watch the kites?"

I took us up through the south end of Berkeley, over the freeway, and down to the water. "When I was your age," I said, "there used to be these weird figures built into the wetlands here. All kinds of them. Snoopy's doghouse, boats, planes. There was one that looked like a jail cell with these giant wooden hands sticking out from between the bars."

On windy days, the short peninsula at the tip of the marina is packed with kite flyers. We'd been out there a few times to fly the little red stunt kite I bought Gene for his birthday one year. Today, a whole flock of kites filled the sky.

"Really?" Gene asked.

"I think so. It seems weird, I guess, now that I'm thinking about it." The kites rose and fell. They swooped at one another and danced. "You won't find this in Cleveland," I said.

"They don't have kites in Cleveland?"

"No," I said. "They probably do. I mean the water, the sun. All this."

After awhile, Gene stopped looking at the kites. I knew we needed a new distraction so I got back on 80 and headed south. At the interchange I went west over the bridge into the city. Late morning traffic was a breeze; in no time the city was behind us and the day had almost started to feel right. We'd made it past the airport when my phone rang. I held the phone in my hand, watched Katie's name blink on the screen for a second before I answered. "Jim," she said, "We're starting to get worried. We don't want to miss our flight."

"We're just taking a drive, talking a little."

"Hi, Mom," Gene said. It was the first thing he'd said in a while.

"Hi, Genie," she said to me. "Try to get back soon, OK, Jim? We're going to leave in an hour."

We pulled off in Redwood City and drove out to the marina where I once took Gene sailing. It was right below the flight path for the airport. We leaned forward to look up through the windshield at the planes. They came in low and loud, floating a little as if they were barely moving at all until they were right on top of us. It felt dangerous, like at any minute a plane could come crashing down, canceling everything out in a wave of water and fiery metal.

"Wow," Gene said.

"That's something," I said. "Take a look at that."

In the marina, the masts of the sailboats rode the wind. They shook and swayed. Flags snapped and then fell limp. Gene rolled his window down. The wind caught at his hair. "I'm going to ride on a plane like that today."

"We'll get back soon," I said. "Enjoy the day, Genie. It's a pretty one."

An hour after Katie's call I pulled into the parking lot of a Best Buy somewhere near San Jose. The cities had started to merge together. The hills got lower, making the sky feel enormous. It was

For Out of the Heart Proceed

like we were in a different state altogether. I closed my eyes and imagined that. Katie called again. "Jim," she said, "please."

"We're fine, Katie. We're having a good time together. Right, Gene?"

"Do I have to go home soon?" Gene asked.

"Robert is calling the police. Just come back." I heard her shush Robert in the background, then his muffled voice asking to speak with me. "I knew you'd try something like this, Jim," Katie said.

When she said that, I understood I'd known that too. "I can do this, Katie," I said and hung up.

It was scorching hot. The asphalt in the parking lot bit at our shins. "I bet you'll be glad to get out of here, Genie. Our kind doesn't do well in these temperatures."

"I like it when it's hot," he said. "I've adapted."

The giant doors slid open as we approached. "See," I said, showing Gene our true robot nature, "we're kings here. Doors open for us." I thought of Ted on the lawn the day before and jerked my arms up and down, beeped a couple times. The robot is lonely. Gene looked up at me, turning his whole body to follow his head. It was a perfect pantomime of a robot.

"Do they have our kind in Cleveland?" Gene asked.

"Affirmative," I said. "We're everywhere."

Gene locked his knees and put his arms straight out in front of him like he was reaching for an idea. We went inside to commune with our kind. A whole wall of televisions was showing the same silent music video. Dancers on the screen moved to an inaudible rhythm. I caught up to my son and together we continued up and down the aisles, listening for a message, some kind of clue to our future on this planet.

Acknowledgments

Thanks to the editors of the following publications, where many of the stories in the book first appeared, often in different form and occasionally under different titles:

"For out of the Heart Proceed" in *Avery*, "Divine Messages" in *Bateau*, "The Dark Is What" in *BULL*, "Spaceport America" in *Corium*, "The Sorry Teds" in *elimae*, "We Cannot Cross the River" in *Everyday Genius*, "Wyoming" in *JMWW*, "Orion," in *Keyhole*, "Africa" in *The Lifted Brow*, "Peafowl" in *Necessary Fiction*, "Family" in *Necessary Fiction* & Best of the Web 2010 (Dzanc), "Ritual" in *notnostrums*, "The Weather Factory" in *Opium*, "How It Was When a Car Caught Fire on the Street outside My House Last Night," "Their Future Gets Brighter the Closer It Gets to the Sun," & "In All the World's Oceans" in *Quick Fiction*, "Delaware," in *Sixth Finch*, "Training Exercise" in *Spork*, "To the World I'll Be Buried" in *Waccamaw*.

I need to thank many people for their help in bringing this book to life. If I tried to list them all, I'd have to fill a whole new book with names. But I'd especially like to thank the following people for their friendship, support, patience and advice:

Chris Bachelder, Noy Holland, Sabina Murray and James Tate; trusted friends and editors who first saw many of these stories and contributed greatly to their improvement, especially Matt Bell, Aaron Burch, Drew Burke, Elizabeth Ellen, Jarrett Haley, Steve Himmer, Adam Koehler, Jennifer & Adam Pieroni and Todd Zuniga; Kevin Murphy and *Dark Sky Books*, in particular Brian Carr who kept me honest and made this book so much better; the compound: David Bartone, Jeff Downey, Kyle Flak, Hilary Plum and Zach Savich; to Michael Kimball, Lindsay Hunter, and Steve Yarbrough for the support and kindness; my kids: Noah, Theo and Ellie; and most of all my wife Anna, my love, my life, my heart.

About the author

Jensen Beach's writing has appeared most recently in *American Short Fiction*, *Fifty-Two Stories*, *Ninth Letter*, *Sou'wester*, and *Witness*, among others. He teaches at the University of Illinois in Urbana-Champaign, where he lives with his family.

Also Available from DARK SKY BOOKS:

January 2008
by Ben Mazer
(*poetry*)

Muted Lines from Someone Else's Memory
by Seth Berg
(*poetry*)

I Have Touched You
by Gregory Sherl
(*fiction*)

Cut Through the Bone
by Ethel Rohan
(*fiction*)

Trees of the Twentieth Century
by Stephen Sturgeon
(*poetry*)

Cowboy Maloney's Electric City
by Michael Bible
(*fiction*)

Hunters & Gamblers
by Ryan Ridge
(*fiction*)

Morocco
by Kendra Grant Malone & Matthew Savoca
(*poetry*)